The Connect's Wife V:

The End

Nako

Dedication:

To the readers who have become like long-lost girlfriends, if I named each and every one of you from Facebook & Instagram that will take up the majority of the book y'all know who you are! And to the beautiful women who sent encouraging words and left reviews on part IV, y'all are the real CONNECT!

So grateful for the support, there aren't enough words to collectively come together to express my gratitude.

Thank you to the squad #TBRS for sharing every link on release day. I'm so grateful and for each of you who read The Connect's Wife series, thank you so much.

Your publisher and your editor are the most important people to a writer, I'm grateful to have the best in the game standing on the left and right sides of me. I know I'm a personal headache, unfortunately this is only the beginning.

(kisses and hugs LOL)

To my friends and family, I love y'all so much and thank you for understanding when I'm rushing you off the phone or not texting back. It's grind time baby!

To Maria Sanchez, thank you for everything, you might think dropping the link to my book in over a hundred different reading groups is something simple since you've been doing it for years, but it literally means EVERYTHING to me because I am so lazy when it comes to promotion! May God bless you in more ways than one.

I hope every person reading this book enjoys it,

With love,

NAKO

The Roundtable Meeting
Miami, Florida
July 20th 2015
Epic Hotel
Ballroom A

The tension in the room was thick. The atmosphere was one that really couldn't be described in one sentence. Farren Knight sat across from Mario Sanchez. She was dressed in a grey pinstripe suit and pumps. She had her hair slicked back in a bun. She couldn't believe that she was missing Noel's soccer championship and as soon as this meeting came to an end she was hopping on the next flight back to Jersey, to celebrate with her family. Farren didn't want to be here and she hoped that it didn't show on her face.

She was amongst the elite of The Cartel. The Roundtable meeting was only held once a year, it was a time for all of the families under the umbrella of The Cartel to celebrate their success, to speak on downfalls and to sometimes promote and demote families or add new members of The Cartel. The Roundtable had been discussed in songs written by various Hip-Hop artists and had been reenacted in several gangster movies and television shows.

The Roundtable was nothing like the *Sopranos* or *The Wire*, this meeting was laidback yet serious. The room was filled with people from all kinds of backgrounds and different ethnicities, men were smoking expensive cigars, drinking Remy and sipping on Champagne. The meeting hadn't begun yet, Farren and Mario were the only ones not socializing. They were too busy texting each other back and forth.

She was so caught up in casually flirting with his ass, that she didn't notice that Greg had taken a seat next to her and Kool on her other side.

"Thanks for looking out sis," Greg told her.

"I didn't," she told him. She nudged Kool and all he did was nod his head to acknowledge her. He looked paranoid and she could tell that he didn't trust anybody here.

To be sitting at a Roundtable meeting was probably a street nigga's dream, so she was going to let him bask in the moment.

"Families, let's come together and get to business," Mr. Bianchi said.

He called the meeting to order about fifteen minutes later. "We have two additional members to the family, Kool and Greg. They will work under one of the families for six months before they are supplied with their own work, so snatch them up while you can," Bianchi joked.

Kool asked, "Work under somebody? That's not what I was told," he said.

"Patience is a virtue," Bianchi told him.

Greg remained quiet. He already know they worked, so he wasn't surprised.

"Moving on to the next order of business. As usual the Sanchez Family have been bringing in tripled the amount of profits as compared to everyone else. Mario, I know your papa is proud, salute," Bianchi said holding his glass up to Mario.

Farren didn't know Mario was getting to it like that. Hell, every time she talked to his ass he was too busy traveling and shopping.

"As you all know we buried our dear Farad, one of my personal buddies, but his daughter has stepped in and has kept the ball rolling. Farren, we are extending your contract for ten years," Bianchi said.

Farren shook her head, "No thank you. I was told this was temporary, I don't even understand why I'm here now honestly," she said.

The Families looked at her in disbelief. Mario shook his head, but Farren didn't care. She wasn't doing this bullshit anymore.

"We will talk after the meeting," he dismissed her.

It really wasn't nothing to talk about, plus she had a flight to catch anyway.

Bianchi continued on going down the report and update list, this went on for about an hour.

"Did I miss anything?" he asked.

An older Italian man whispered in his ear and Farren saw Mr. Bianchi roll his eyes.

"Unfortunately, we have to vote to lift the ban on Christian Knight, it's in the bylaws. I vote no," he said quickly.

"Let's write it down," someone shouted.

"We are all grown men, it's yes or no," another person shouted.

"Okay, okay. Let's do this, starting right here Salvador… Yes or no and let's take it around," he said.

"Yes," Salvador Gatiano said.

"Yes," Luis Diaz spoke.

"No," Kimberly Lohan answered, Farren was surprised.

"Yes," Jose Vargas answered.

"No," Hector Martinez answered.

"Yes," Omar Jackson answered.

"Hell no, I hate that black cunt," Raul Caballero grunted.

Mario looked at Farren and she looked away, Greg peeped it too. "No," Mario Sanchez responded.

"Yes," Meir Abergil stated.

"No," Shorty Sinaloa answered.

"Yes, I made good money with Christian," Emma Bastidos stated honestly. Know her, she was probably fucking Christian.

"No" Andrew O'Meyer responded.

Greg answered, "No," and surprisingly, Farren was not surprised.

"No response," she told The Families.

"You have to vote sweetheart, husband or not," Mr. Bianchi told her with an evil smile.

Farren allowed her mind to travel back to so many different memories, she didn't even know what to say. Christian had brought her heaven on earth, then dragged her through hell and back.

His face flashed through her mind, him in that jail…away from his children.

Then she thought of the nights she laid in bed, crying her eyes out, missing him, wanting him back, and blowing him up. Begging him to come home and be with her and he would curse her out and block her number.

Farren then thought how he came through for her or so many occasions, Christian loved her so much, and that she believed in her heart.

If he came home, would he give her the divorce she had asked for twice or he would fight to work on their marriage?

Would she take him back?

Did he even deserve her?

Farren loved him, well she used to love him. Damn, did she still love him?

Was Christian Knight still considered an important factor in her life?

Farren thought back to the first time they made love, the first time she gave him head, their first argument, first fuck, first everything.

Christian was a different type of man and it takes a very different, yet strong and confident woman to love a man like him.

Farren was literally torn in between the two, stuck in the past. She didn't know whether to let his ass rot or to give him the chance to redo his life again.

Would she give him the boot and demand for a divorce.

Would he be The CONNECT again?

"Farren? Yes or No?" Mr. Bianchi asked once more.

The Connect's Wife V

Introduction

Farren wrote in her diary, the morning of the funeral:

Never ever in a million years did I think I would lose him. I loved him, he was really my everything. How was this fair? How was I supposed to wake up tomorrow knowing that he wouldn't be there? The tears that cascaded down my face wouldn't stop, every time I wiped them away more came. It hurt me to know that this was my reality, I prayed for my strength, I prayed that I would be okay one day. Man, love is so real and I was sure that I wouldn't experience that type of love ever again, it was bottled up, locked up, hidden and discarded. Although it had been tarnished just a little, it was still delicate to me. Memories keep replaying in my head and I find myself laughing then crying, I find myself hurt and angry, sad then happy. I wonder how he expects me to feel. I wonder before he took his last breathe, did he think of me?

I just wonder did he ever love me as much as I loved him.

Chapter One

Farren was at a complete loss of words, she literally had nothing to say. She was stuck, frozen, her eyes searched for an answer in Mr. Bianchi, Mario, Greg, Kool and the other people in the room. This day would be talked about forever, Farren Knight turned her back on her estranged husband. She was sure that someone in the room would leak the vote and it would slowly find its way to Christian Knight. In her dreams he would visit her and taunt her, he might even send someone to kill her. How could Farren leave her husband, her once favorite person in the entire world, her children's father, the man who brought life back into her body after Dice…how could she leave him in there to rot?

"Farren?" Mr. Bianchi shouted.

"Yes!" she shouted back. Everyone gasped, "I mean no, I vote no," she said.

Mr. Bianchi rolled his eyes. "What is your fucking answer, yes or no?" he asked.

She bit her lip and tapped her fingers on the table, Farren had a beautiful life with Jonte. She was completely over Christian, so whether he was home or not, it wouldn't affect her life. Because her life didn't include Christian Knight at all, she was completely over him.

Farren voted, "Yes."

The votes continued.

Kool voted, "Yes."

Jeff voted, "Yes."

And of course, the verdict read, Christian Knight would soon be released from prison.

"Does this mean, he's back in?" Greg asked.

"Hell no, not as long as I sit at the head of this table," Mr. Bianchi roared.

The meeting was then adjourned and some people were delighted and some were full of bitterness. Farren didn't know how to feel.

Kool asked her, "You good shawty?"

"Why did you vote yes?" she asked out of curiosity.

"Prison ain't the place to be, there are people in there who wish it was that easy to get out," he told her.

"Thank you," Farren told him, kindly.

Farren didn't even look in Greg's direction, she would be telling Christian Knight with no hesitation that his best friend and brother turned on him. Folks let money cloud their judgement and it wasn't cool at all. Greg was a disappointment in Farren's eyes.

She motioned to Mario that she would call him later and Farren exited the ballroom. Bianchi called out to her, "Farren, come see me next week."

She didn't even bother to turn around and acknowledge him, Farren was trying to fly back to Jersey in time to celebrate with her daughter. She was just praying the jet was gassed up and ready to go. Farren planned on buying her own, once the money from her father's insurance policy came in.

Farren just couldn't believe Greg, she just couldn't. She called Kennedy and told her to tell Christian, that everything was handled.

Farren knew she had to tell Jonte before he heard it on the streets, it was only right.

She made her way home, and her heart was extremely heavy. As much as she wanted to act like things were going to be okay, Farren knew everything was about to change. The only thing she wasn't able to predict was whether it was about to be a positive or negative outcome.

Farren worried that her perfect little fairytale was about to be ruined by the evil character in all of the fables. The evil character was her estranged husband, Christian Knight.

Christian believed that Farren belonged to him. He never once considered the fact that he had left her, betrayed her, and embarrassed her in front of family, friends and even business associates. Christian didn't consider her feelings at first, nor did he care how she was feeling or how she handled their break up. Christian didn't wipe not one tear or even apologize for his indiscretions, he was unconcerned with her well-being.

But now that Asia, the supposed to be love of his life, was out of the picture. Christian's attention was back on Farren. Oh the irony. People back in the day used to say never leave the one you love for the one you like because the one you like will leave you for one they love. And if that wasn't true, then who knows what was. It was just like a man, a black man with power and money, to want to crawl back to what they knew was the best thing that ever happened to them. Christian didn't appreciate all the kind things that Farren did before when he was sleeping with other women and parlaying them around town without a care in the world. Farren didn't cross Christian's mind when he was blocking her calls and lying to her about his multiple trips to Atlanta.

Christian was unconcerned with his wife and their children, but now that he would be soon released he was eager to get his once tight-knit family back together. They were all that he had and he would do anything to live under one roof all again. Christian liked Jonte, he was a stand-up dude. However, if he didn't let Farren go in peace, he had no problem killing his ass.

Everyone was sleep when she got home and she knew she shouldn't have went to the stupid Roundtable meeting. It was almost as if she was forced to go.

Farren showered and met Jonte in bed, "I missed you," she whispered in his ear. She wanted to wake him up, Farren needed to be held and comforted, right about now.

She needed to hear Jonte tell her that everything was okay and that he was going to protect her from the storm that was brewing for sure.

"Miss you too baby," he said, yawning.

"Did Noel win?" she asked.

"Nah, but she played a good game. I promised her tomorrow we can do whatever she wanted. She cried herself to sleep," Jonte told his girl, with his eyes still closed.

"Can you hold me?" she asked, sadly.

Jonte turned over and looked in her eyes. "What's wrong bae?" he asked.

"I'm stuck…with them forever. It's no getting out," she told him, crying.

Jonte said nothing because he already knew what was up from the beginning, which is why he warned her, but she was stubborn and hard-headed and didn't listen.

Jonte had plenty of opportunities to join The Cartel, but the risks were too high. Your life, your family's life, and the people who depended on you to eat lives were all in the hands of The Cartel. Jonte wasn't a greedy man, and money didn't make him happy. Before Farren, he was content with his two bedroom condo that he paid eleven hundred dollars a month and his used Audi. Jonte wasn't flashy and he wore a white t-shirt and jeans every day. He was a simple nigga who tried his best to stay off the radar of the police and most importantly the Feds.

"We will work through this," Jonte told her.

"Christian is coming home, they voted today. It's just too much going on all at once. Oh and Greg was voted in as well. Shit is crazy," she ran him down today's events.

"Damn," Jonte responded.

"How did Greg get that high up without Christian?" he asked.

That was something that Farren hadn't thought about, and it was something that she definitely planned on getting to the bottom of soon.

All she wanted was to be held by her man all night until she fell asleep. Farren wished that when she woke up her life was back to normal, or that she could click her heels two or three times and her father would be back on this earth. But she knew none of that shit was possible, so she sucked it up, putting her feelings to the side and mentally prepared to deal with what was in front of her due to the primary fact that she really had no choice.

The next morning, she sat at the bar in her kitchen, drinking coffee and journaling. Jonte snuck up on her and kissed her cheek. "Why are you up so early? Did you get any sleep?" he asked.

She shook her head, "No, not really. I'm good though. I have a busy day ahead of me," she told her fiancé.

"What does your day consist of ma, any time for me?" he asked. Farren turned around and placed her hands around Jonte's neck. "Dinner on me tonight. I just have a few errands to run and I promised Mari that we can meet for lunch," she added, rolling her eyes.

Jonte smiled, "I love you for that baby, she misses her best friend," he told her. Farren wasn't stunting shit Jonte was saying. She was only going to eat with Mari because she was tired of her texting and calling her day in and day out.

"When do you report back?" he asked.

"I'm not sure, I'll have to fly out to Miami soon though," she told Jonte.

Farren was hoping that Jeff didn't come calling her phone at least for another month, she was pushing for two months, but she already knew that wasn't about to happen.

Farren couldn't wait to gossip with Mario about what happened after she left the meeting, she knew he had the tea.

"I'm about to go get dressed, what you doing today?" Farren asked.

"Not much, take Noel wherever she wanna go," he said.

"Well, we can all go together. I just need to hit the salon, nail shop, grocery store, Laundromat, pay some bills then lunch with your sister in law," she ran down her schedule to him.

"Man hell nah, we're gonna be back home by then," Jonte told his fiancée.

"Wait on meeeeee," she whined.

"I'll let you know," Jonte told her, and smacked her on the butt before she walked away.

Not less than an hour later, Farren was out the door. As soon as she left the salon and hit the nail shop, she would be able to say she was feeling herself, but until then she was looking real deranged.

At the red light, she scanned her phone for text messages and missed calls. Kool had hit her line, "What the hell he want?" she said aloud.

The phone rang twice before he answered, "What it do?" his voice came through the phone.

"Hi, this is Farren returning your call," she said in her most professional tone.

He laughed, "Where are you?" he asked.

"Home, Jersey. How may I help you?" Farren asked.

"Come see me soon."

"Uhh, about what?"

"You'll have to see," he flirted.

"Okay. Umm Kool, I have a fiancé and three children. Whatever you're looking for, you won't be able to find it with me. Sorry boo boo," she checked him real quick.

He busted out laughing, "Girl, you are extremely too funny for me. None of that, you're not even my type."

Farren got silent, not his type? Tuh! Please.

"Well, if it's pertaining to business, you can contact Jeff to schedule an appointment."

"Cool," he said and disconnected the call.

Kool was on some bullshit and she didn't even know why he called because he never just came out and said it. She made her way to the beauty salon ready to be revitalized.

After handling all of her business and running her errands, Farren mentally prepared herself to meet with her 'best friend' Mari. Farren was trying to remember or relocate when she stopped fucking with Mari, or when she started feeling some type of way about her lack of ambition.

Mari's lack of independency bothered Farren, she had always been a go-getter. There was never a time where Farren wasn't a hustler. She kept a job, or two. Some people were natural born hustlers and preferred to make their own income and hours while there were others who paved their own way to stack their bread. Either way it goes, money is money, and it all spent the same no matter how you woke up and made it.

Mari didn't do either of those, there was no way possible that she spent millions and millions and millions of dollar in a matter of three years. Farren didn't believe and Jonte damn sure didn't. It would have been somewhat understandable had her house or cars been paid off, or she invested it into some stocks, but the dumb bitch didn't even do that.

Mari shopped and smoked weed all day every day, the only thing that she would never take away from her was that she was a damn good mother to her kids. Mari would lay down and die before her kids went without, Johan had always spoiled them rotten and she definitely continued the tradition.

"Hey girl," Mari said, once Farren approached the table.

"Hi, sorry I'm late. I've been paying bills all day," she told her friend.

"It's cool, I'm still on my first margarita," she told her.

Farren didn't respond, she was texting Jonte to see where they were and what they were doing, she was ready to get to her family.

"So how have you been? And sorry about your dad," she said.

"Staying busy, and thanks girl. I'm good, I'm just happy he's not suffering."

"I feel you on that, I remember when my daddy died. Girllll... Whew, I went through it."

Comment [A]: This doesn't make any sense. Wouldn't both of these mean that they were entrepreneurs and finding their own way? Are you trying to say people climbed the corporate ladder to pave their way?

Farren ordered a drink and an appetizer. She wasn't really hungry, but didn't wanna be rude and not order anything.

"How are the kids?" Farren asked. Mari's face lit up when she went to talk about her kids and everything they had going on.

Farren made it her business to spend more time with her girls, especially since they were getting older.

"Did Jonte give you that check from us?" she asked.

Mari rolled her eyes, "Hmm hmm, I was behind on a few bills, but yeah I got it. Thanks," she said dryly.

"You're very welcome. So what do you have planned? Did you look into some locations for your daycare?" she asked.

"Nah, not yet," she said, nonchalantly.

"Okay…When are you getting started? Do you need a realtor?" she questioned.

"Farren, I just wanted to eat some good food and get drunk, like we used to do, please don't start damn" she said loudly.

"Mari, please open your eyes. Your husband is DEAD, okay? He's not coming back. You need to get on your shit for real," she told her.

"I'm sorry that I don't have the balls to travel the world and risk my freedom for some motherfuckers that don't give a damn about me. My bad, okay," she yelled.

Farren's breathing increased, "Don't you ever in your life repeat that again and news flash, that lil money is nothing to me because I have my own," she told her.

Their food was placed in front of them but Farren Knight had lost her appetite.

"Jonte said whenever I need something he got me, and I need some money. That lil raggedy million dollars will be gone by the end of the summer, I already know," she said.

"Mari, what is it? Does money burn a whole in your pocket or something? Like please let me know what the fuck you're doing with your money?" Farren asked, but she really wanted an answer to her question.

"None of your damn business. Like I said, my brother Jonte said he got me," she said with an attitude.

Farren couldn't do nothing but shake her head, she was so irritated that she couldn't even place the spoon to her mouth to eat her beans and rice.

"Why don't you wanna work? You're from the hood, I don't understand your lack of hustle," she attempted to try to get on the same level as her to comprehend where she was coming from and why she carried herself the way she did.

"I lost my husband! I lost my fucking husband, my everything. My lifeline, my best friend, my cheerleader, my life. I lost my husband, okay. You will never understand how that feels or what I'm going through. NEVER!" she said, with tears streaming down her face.

Farren was thankful that the area they were seated wasn't filled with too many patrons because Mari had been drinking and she was a tad bit emotional.

"In case you forgot, I lost the first person that I ever really loved. Shit, I haven't loved right since Dice died. He was my first in a million areas. Okay? And worse than that, I saw him fucking die in front of me and there was nothing I could do about it. So bitch don't tell me what I don't know," she snapped back.

Damn Mari had pissed her off, no one knew how she empty and miserable she felt after losing Dice. The thing that bothered Farren the most about death was that people moved on. Time was supposed to heal all wounds, and they say that one day you're going to be okay, and that you will smile again.

However, since Dice's death, Farren knew she hadn't been the same. She missed every single thing about him. Dice was the right amount of controlling and submissive, he was everything she needed him to be and she was lacking that, "you're all I ever want in life" feeling.

She wiped the tears from the face as she thought about him and a few of her favorite memories flashed through her mind. Dice was everything to her, damn she missed him.

"Do these jeans look good on me?" she asked Dice.

"Yeah, they do. Let's go," he rushed her. They had been at the mall for hours and he wasn't planning on spending all day with his young girl, there was money to be made.

"Are you sure boo? Cus they look a lil baggy in the butt if you ask me," she said.

Dice took a deep breath, "Baby, I got stuff to do. I'm not trying to be in New York all day," he finally told her.

"Oh excuse me then. Well let me get dressed, sorry for wasting your day," Farren said sadly. She didn't know that after the mall their time together was ending. She just knew that they were going to spend the entire day together, spending his hard-earned drug money and then making sweet love all night.

Farren and Dice had recently started having sex and boy, she was missing out! Dice had been blowing her mind every single day. He was sliding through her crib every morning after he dropped his kids at daycare and before he went home to his nagging ass wife.

Dice was trying to slow their sex down. He really enjoyed Farren and didn't want to grow tired of her, which he knew could happen. Dice genuinely liked Farren, although he always drove an hour and sometimes two to spend time with her so no one would see him, he still really cared about her. Which is why he hadn't fucked her in a few weeks. Dice knew his lil baby was in heat, she had sucked his dick the entire way to the mall. Farren was hoping that she could wake up his hormones, he pull over on the side of the highway and fuck her brains out, but Dice did nothing but encourage her to continue sucking it, "just like that".

Dice felt Farren's mood change, he opened the curtain and saw his little baby naked and putting her clothes back on.

"Looking good Snook," he admired her, licking his lips. That was the lil nickname that he gave her.

"Get out," she told him.

"Why?" he asked, coming closer to her. The dressing room wasn't but so big, but Dice got tired of sitting in the chair waiting on her to get dressed.

"You gotta get back remember, so let me get dressed QUICKLY," she snapped.

Dice couldn't do nothing but shake his head. When Farren had an attitude she didn't do anything to hide it, she wanted you to know that she had an issue with you. Most girls, who were talking to a nigga with money, would answer the phone every time the dude called and always be available.

Uh no, not Farren. She talked to Dice when she felt like it, and if she had plans with her best friend or if she was studying for a test, there was no cancelling just to chill with Dice. That nigga was on her time, ALWAYS.

"Shut the fuck up with all that," Dice told her, whipping his dick out.

Farren heard his jeans being zipped down, "We are in a dressing room!" she whispered.

"I don't care, I want that pussy now," he told her, smothering her face with kisses. Farren wanted to protest, but she wasn't. She had been playing with her pussy, going three fingers deep because she had been so horny lately. Dice had not been coming through with that dope dick like he was in the beginning and she was beginning to get worried. Was it dry? Was she not as experienced as his wife or his other females?

"Hmm damn, I miss my pussy," he whispered in her ear, as he stroked her real slow from behind.

Farren took deep breaths, and she mentally prepared herself for Dice's length and width, it was riDICKolous!

"You feel that dick, don't you?" he asked, pulling her head back, and biting her neck.

Farren closed her eyes and embraced it all, she had really, really missed him. Farren knew the sounds of her pussy was being heard behind the curtain in the dressing room, but she didn't care. If this was when Dice wanted to bless her, then hell, she had to get it how she could.

Minutes later, he sped up his pace and brought the both of them to a silent climax.

Farren used one of the blouses she'd tried on to clean the both of them up. Dice kissed her lips one more time before he made sure the coast was clear for them to exit the dressing room.

"You do like me right?" she asked, once they got back in the car and was headed back to Hardy Projects.

"Yeah baby, you know that. Come on now," he said.

"I feel like you do, but I don't know. I barely see you now," she told him.

"Getting money baby. I gotta keep you looking fly," he told her, grabbing at her chin trying to mack and keep his eyes on the road at the same time.

"It's not about being fly. I just want quality time with you," she snapped.

Dice smacked his lips, "Don't start, I'ma do better, I promise."

Farren turned in his direction. "Is that your word?" she wanted clarification because Dice was one smooth motherfucker.

"Fa sho, you're who I wanna be with when I'm not in the streets and that's on everything." He winked.

Farren snapped back into present day. Damn, they ain't make real niggas no more, they were a rare breed.

"Look, yes you miss your boyfriend or whatever he was, who was MARRIED to someone else, but we're not gon go there. Until you lose your husband, you don't know what I'm going through," she said matter-of-factly.

Farren didn't even bother arguing, it was obvious that this bitch was delusional.

She took one more sip of her drink and stood to her feet, "Farren, I didn't mean to make you upset," Mari stated.

"Oh girl, I'm not upset. I got other shit to do with my time, the tab is on you though," she told her and dipped.

Farren refused to treat a miserable bitch to dinner, Mari could sit there alone and entertain herself. One topic that she was extremely sensitive about was Dice. You can speak on Chrissy leaving her all day, but DICE...don't speak on Dice. That was her man, no matter how people perceived it to be. He loved her and she loved him.

Farren checked her phone and she had a message from Jeff saying report to Miami Monday and Atlanta before the end of next week.

She couldn't do nothing but laugh, that nigga Kool moved real fast. She called his phone, "Ummm, you owe me for making me having to rush to Atlanta knowing your ass don't want shit," she said.

"Business is business, never take it personal shawty," he told her coolly.

"Whatever," she teased him.

"I'm going to show you a good time when you get here too."

"We will see. I drink patron," she told him ahead of time.

"Got that on deck already," he said.

"Well, I'll let you go. See you soon sir," she told him.

It made Farren feel good deep down on the inside for her to know that she still had a little swag about her. The lil young niggas was at her constantly, but her fiancé had her on lock. She loved every single thing about him.

"Bae, where are you?" she asked.

"Hardy," he said

"Doing what?"

"Shooting dice."

"Hmm okay," she told him and hung the phone up. Jonte didn't even bother to call back, he already knew Farren was about to pull up.

Jonte told Trina, "You need to go on and leave, my baby mama is on the way up here."

Trina rolled her eyes, "I'm not going anywhere," she popped at the mouth.

Jonte just shook his head. He was up in the game, so there was no way he was about to stop what he was doing. Farren had already whooped Trina's ass once, if she hadn't learned her lesson the first time, then that was on her.

Not even thirty minutes later, her Bond fragrance invaded the alley.

"I like your hair like this." Jonte kissed her lips, and ran his hand through her curls.

"I feel like an old lady. Wasup Spider?" Farren spoke to Jonte's best friend and he threw her a head nod back.

"How long you been out here? Where the kids?" she asked quietly, not wanting anyone in their business.

"Noel and Morgan are in there with your mama. Mike is at the neighbor's house," he told her.

"You want me to take them with me?" she asked.

"It don't matter baby. You ate?" he asked, before Farren could answer his question. Jonte was blowing on his dice and tossing it across the ground.

Farren felt someone's eyes on her and she looked around, but didn't see a bunch of niggas as they were all too focused on the money they had invested in the dice game.

Farren hated that Jonte spent so much time shooting dice. It got on her nerves and it was unsafe, a dice game could go left real quick.

Jonte held on to her waist, "How was lunch?" he asked. She blushed at how attentive he was attempting to be while trying to pay attention to the dice game as well, she wouldn't be at here long. She just wanted to see her baby's face.

"Horrible, I think our friendship has come to an end," she told him.

"We are all family, Farren," Jonte's face frowned up.

"Never said we wasn't." She kissed him back and walked off in the direction of her mother's apartment. Farren was looking and feeling like money. Despite how tight her curls were she was hoping that they would fall soon, so she could really pop out.

"That hoe old as fuck, Tae ain't really fucking with her," a voice that wanted to be heard, but apparently not being seen.

Farren kept walking, she didn't talk to people who she couldn't even see.

"Girl, you better stop letting him play you," someone else said.

"I'm not the one being played, it's her," and that's when she knew it was that same young bitch from last time.

Farren turned around and that's when she saw them sitting on the balcony on the third floor. Farren never took her designer frames off to address the peasant, "You got something that you need to say?" she asked.

"Get your old ass on," Trina said.

"Old, rich, fly and way fresher than you," Farren said and kept walking.

"I'm sucking and fucking your man more than you is, so fresh ain't got nothing to do with good pussy," she yelled from over the porch.

Okay that's where the line was crossed, but she wasn't the problem, her nigga was.

Jonte had already heard the commotion and was pissed he had to pull out the game.

"Go home," he told her, once they met in the middle of the Courtyard.

"Get your bitch. The only reason that I'm not nutting the fuck up right now, is on the strength of my kids being at my mama's house," she told him through clenched teeth.

"Man, go home, everything is good," he brushed her off.

"Good? Jonte, no the fuck it's not. Why do you keep fucking this girl? She look ratchet as hell, that's what you want? Her or me?" Farren asked, elevating her voice just a little bit so he can get her point loud and clear.

"Farren, I'm not doing this with you right here. I said go home," he told her and she heard the seriousness in his voice, so she deaded the issue…for now.

Her mother was already bringing the kids through the Courtyard. "They was sleep?" Jonte asked.

He always so concerned with the well-being of his daughters, "Yeah knocked out, Jonte go on home and be with your family. It ain't nothing out here, but drama and bullshit," Ms. Nakia told him.

It was people like Jonte that made enough money to leave the projects in which he grew up alone, but he felt the need to always pop up and come back. Jonte was hood rich and when he got with Farren, his status and income increased tremendously. She broadened his horizons and showed him numerous ways to get his money right, but Jonte loved the hood. He loved the BBQ's, the dog fights and dice games. Jonte could be found in Hardy 24/7.

He ignored his future mother in law. "I'll be home in a minute. I'm right behind you, bae," he told Farren.

"Ma, I'll call you later," she told her mother, ignoring her lying, cheating, sorry as, baby daddy.

Farren got the girls buckled in to their seats and got in her car. She looked in her rearview mirror to see if Jonte was headed to his car as well, but he went back to his dice game as if her feelings or her respect was not just tarnished.

It was obvious that he didn't care, or that he thought she wasn't going anywhere, the sad part was Farren couldn't bear being alone again. She didn't want to ever have to cry herself to sleep again. Farren didn't know what possessed Jonte to think it was acceptable for him to fuck hoes. She wasn't one of them bitches who spoke so highly of their nigga coming home to them every night, so who cared what he did in the streets. Nah, won't be Farren, especially if she was all you needed and plus some.

Farren wondered what she did so wrong or in what areas did she lack… Why did niggas constantly feel the need to cheat on her?

She prayed that she was knocked out sleep when Jonte got home, whenever that would be. It seemed as if when she was away he claimed to miss her so much, but when she was at home, his ass stayed away.

Farren contemplated for a few minutes, damn was she getting played? Jonte wouldn't play her, right? Or would he?

She had to get her feelings out of the situation and look at it from all different angles.

Farren didn't want to think that Jonte never loved her or really fucked with her as he always claimed he did.

She took a deep breath and pulled out of the parking lot, she needed to get home to her wine and get her mind together.

"Where is my daddy?" Morgan asked.

"He's going to meet us at home. Did y'all eat? Are y'all hungry?" Farren asked.

"We're good ma," Noel told her.

Farren laughed, Noel reminded her of Carren so much. She really missed her daughter, there wasn't a day went by that she didn't think about her daughter.

"Okay boo," she said. Farren put in a Beyoncé cd, the girls and her rode home jamming to all of their favorite songs.

"Y'all go and take y'all baths then we can watch some movies. When is Mike coming home?" she asked.

"I'm already back," her son yelled from his room.

"Come hug your mama," she yelled back.

Minutes later, her son came into the kitchen where Farren was putting some cookies in the oven for the girls.

"Hey ma," he said, hugging her.

"Hey big boy, you're getting big. Michael, I don't like this haircut at all." She frowned her nose up.

Michael had this new thing where he didn't like to comb his hair out, it was real nappy at the top and shaved low in the back. Ugh, she hated it.

"The ladies do." He winked at her and ran off.

Farren didn't even want to think about girls looking at her only boy, she was not having that shit no time soon.

Farren sipped her wine, sitting in the corner of her living room in the most comfortable chair ever.

Jonte had so much explaining to do it was ridiculous. She wasn't with the shit at all and she would not be disrespected for a second time. Christian had done enough of that to last her a lifetime.

Farren's mind went to her estranged husband, and she wondered was her life about to change once he got home. She prayed that they could come to a few mutual agreements, and possibly co-parent in peace. It was sad that Christian was coming home and she could finally get her divorce papers signed, but now she was very hesitant in marrying Jonte. If he was having problems keeping his dick to himself, it's no telling what was going to happen once they said I do. Bitches loved married niggas. It was something about talking to a man who wanted you but couldn't really have you as much as they wanted to because of the limitations of a marriage.

Farren thanked God for deliverance. She used to think it was acceptable to be in love, super in love with a married man. She didn't care that Dice was married because in her mind she felt like if he didn't respect his marriage or his vows, then hell, she wouldn't either.

She was the young dumb girl a very long time ago, but thirty something years later baby, you had her fucked up. Those days were over.

Farren and the girls watched *Frozen* and *Dreamgirls*, before she knew it, the girls were knocked out. Farren had fallen asleep right with them, wine mixed with stress was the perfect concoction for good sleep.

"Come on boo boo" Farren heard Jonte, her eyes fluttered open and she saw Jonte picking up Noel and Morgan in both of his arms.

Farren yawned, she cut the television off and gathered the mess that they made. They had a lot of fun tonight decorating cookies, making sundaes and then watching movies.

Farren was wiping down the counter when Jonte came from behind her kissing her neck and tugging at her waist, trying to pull her pants down.

"If you don't have a condom, then you need to get back," she told him.

"A rubber? Since when?" he asked, super shocked.

"I'm not fucking you no more, without one. I have kids and I like my life. I won't risk my health for you," she told him and walked off.

"Just come out and say whatever you wanna say, or ask whatever you gotta ask," he shouted.

"Don't raise your voice, OUR children are sleeping," she said, since Jonte didn't like when she said "my".

"Wasup man, why are you on some bullshit all the time?" he asked.

"Bullshit? You think that it's okay for you to fuck bitches in my face, like really Jonte? Come the fuck on," she yelled.

"Farren, that girl is not important. My heart is with you and you know that. It's just some shit that shouldn't be explained," he told her.

"Is this real? Oh no, this shit is not real. Jonte, really? She's not important? You're fucking her and she flaunts it in my face every chance she gets. I beat her ass once and I'm not doing it again. When did you start fucking her anyway? Why are you even cheating on me? I don't understand," she asked.

"It's a nut and that shit don't mean nothing to me at all. Like nothing baby, I promise it don't."

"That doesn't make it okay. Do you know how many niggas wanna fuck me? Wanna fly me out to see them? Plenty. But I'm with you. I could never open my legs for another. That's called loyalty," she let him know.

"Look, I'm tired of having this conversation. I'm horny," he told her.

"Oh well, you should have spent the night in Hardy then. I'm not fucking you without a condom," Farren told him for the second time and went to her room.

Not three seconds later was the alarm chiming which told her that he left.

She couldn't even shed a tear. This won't be the first time a man walked out on her, but it would be the last. Farren wasn't with the bullshit any more, she just wasn't.

Chapter Two

Christian

"Thank you for coming to get me, I really appreciate it," Christian told his sister. It was sad that he had no one else to call. Everyone had turned their backs on him. Christian was sure that the news had spread through The Cartel that he was being released, but he damn sure didn't expect it to be this soon.

In less than three weeks from when the vote was done, he was packing the few letters he did receive over the time he had spent in prison and was walking through the gates of freedom.

Christian had a few things he needed to do today, he was hoping his sister would just take him to his house so he can handle his business.

"Did you get my keys and stuff from Farren?" he asked.

"You don't wanna go see mama first?" she asked, with her face turned up.

"Look Chloe, I'm grateful for you holding me down while I was away. As soon as I get my business and stuff together, I will be handing you a check. But I'm grown and I will be going to see my mama, after I take a hot bath, smoke a blunt, have a glass of Remy and eat all of my favorite foods," he checked her.

Chloe couldn't do nothing but turn her head back to the road, and continue on their journey home. Her brother was back, Christian Knight was back.

He grabbed her phone without asking and scrolled through her contacts trying to get to Kennedy's number. He saw that she had a number saved under "choco candy" and almost threw up in his mouth. His sister was a lil secret freak.

Christian called Kennedy, he was hoping she answered. He didn't have time to play games with Farren ass.

"Hi auntie, did you go get Uncle Chrissy?" she asked, as soon as she answered the phone.

"Yeah, she got me, niece. How are you? And thank you for everything, I'll put some money into your account tomorrow," Christian told his niece.

"I'm good uncle Chrissy. I'm just happy you're home," she said proudly. It felt good that she was able to do something for him since he had done so much for her ever since she was a little girl. She had a gay daddy along with a crazy mama and Kennedy could have come out all wrong, but she was a perfectly normal and educated woman who had recently got married and was now waiting on her the arrival of her first child.

"Me too, kiddo. Do me a favor and call Farren on three-way? She doesn't answer Chloe's calls." he asked.

"Okay, hold on," she told him.

Christian hummed one of his alma mater's chants under his breath, he was just thinking of all the people he wanted to kill when he was locked away. For the first few months, Christian was full of anger, bitterness and resentment. It wasn't until he started doing some serious meditation when he realized he was the one to blame the entire time, he got too comfortable and felt like his position couldn't be taken from him. Christian once humble demeanor was replaced with entirely too much pride.

Christian had already acknowledged all of his flaws. He was so focused now, a bitch wouldn't even be able to lay up with him. Christian was fucking and ducking them, he had a few things on his agenda this week, to get his life back together. But come next week, he was flying to Miami, him and Bianchi needed to have a talk.

He decided to let Asia have her life, he really loved her. She was just caught up in love with another nigga, he didn't fault her for that. However, if he ever came across that pussy ass nigga, it was a wrap for his life.

Christian didn't know what he planned on doing with Greg. Half of him wanted them to just smoke a cigar and talk about the good ol days and the remainder of him wanted to murk his ass in his sleep, only because he did some sneaky shit by getting ghost and not even sending a sign to him in prison to say 'hey brother I got you, I'm here when you get out'. He said nothing. Christian's right hand man, brother and best friend, turned his back completely on him and he really didn't know how he felt about that.

Christian planned on spending some quality time with his children. Man, he wanted to be the best father that he could be. He loved his kids more than anything in this world and it pained him to have missed out on so many of their important achievements in life, but he promised to not miss another. He didn't get to be there for them when Carren died, and he planned on taking them to her gravesite when he went to visit her, his sister and father.

As for Farren, she could stay with her broke ass nigga. Farren was too Hollywood for him now. Christian always secretly liked the hood side of Farren, but now her mouth was too fly and she had forgotten who the fuck he was. Nevertheless, he planned on reminding her, the first time she got out of line with him.

"Hi, Kenn-Kenn," Farren's voice came over the line. Christian couldn't do nothing but blush a little, he hadn't heard her voice in a lil minute.

"Hi auntie…"Christian cut Kennedy off.

"Come get me, from my sister's house," he said.

"Chrissy?" she asked.

"The one and only. I've got some errands to run and bring that stuff," he told her.

"I have stuff to do today. What about Wednesday?" she asked.

Christian chuckled, "Farren, I'll have Chloe text you the address, be there in an hour," he said and hung the phone up.

Yeah, he and Farren was going to have to talk, and a very long it will be.

*****

Farren

"Girl, I cannot believe this nigga," Farren said. She was still staring at her phone in disbelief.

She knew he was coming home, but she assumed that Bianchi was going to take his time contacting the judges; apparently not. This was one of those situations when Farren wished her father was still alive, so he could tell her what was about to happen next.

"Well, I guess I'm cutting our girls' day short," Farren told Kim, who flew to New York just to shop with her friend. They always had a good time together, it never failed.

Farren was on her third mimosa and was feeling herself. She went and got some extensions, twenty-eight inches to be exact, and her hair dyed black with a middle part. Her lashes and brows were popping as well. Farren was dressed sexily in a tangerine halter jumpsuit and Givenchy wedges.

"Awww booooo, is he out for real?" she asked.

"Girl, I don't know what's going on, honestly," she told Kim.

Farren thought to call Jonte to give him a heads up that she would be acting as Christian's chauffeur for today, but decided against it. Their relationship was extremely strained right now and Farren didn't know if she cared to fix it right about now.

"You got the tab?" Farren asked, as she stood.

"Girl get out of here. I'm probably about to fly to Miami, I'm horny," she giggled.

"I'm trying to get like you," Farren teased.

"Girl, Christian Knight go on and let that man put it in your life one good time," she told her, standing up to join her friend so they could leave together.

"Kim, never… Christian will never ever in his life even lick this pussy again," Farren told her.

"Hmm hmm honey, we will see. Y'all were married for how long?" she asked.

"Fifteen happy years, until he started cheating, and we're still married…unfortunately." Farren rolled her eyes.

"Never say never," she told her friend.

"He hurt me to the core." Farren shook her head. There were a lot of things that she felt like were acceptable to forgive in relationships and even marriage, but Christian had crossed so many lines to the point of no possible reconciliation ever.

Plus she had Jonte and had a child with him, Farren would be trifling as hell to ever consider Christian again.

She got in Jonte's Audi and typed in the address that Chloe had sent to her phone. She didn't know that Chloe stayed in the neighborhood up the street from her, wow all this time.

She honked the horn a few times and put the car in park.

Minutes later, Christian Knight appeared coming from the garage and he slid into the passenger's seat.

"Look, this is a nice neighborhood, don't come over here being ghetto," he told her.

She rolled her eyes and turned her music back up, louder than it was before. Christian turned the music down.

"I'm hungry," he told her.

"What do you want to eat?" she asked.

"EVERYTHING, but I'll start off with Ruth's Chris," he told her, rubbing his stomach.

Farren laughed, Christian was about to turn all the muscle he gained right into fat.

She headed in the direction of his favorite steakhouse, he didn't want to hear music. Christian was taking in everything in sight. Farren assumed he had missed the little things.

"How does it feel to be out?" she asked him.

"After I eat and get high, I can answer that question for you," he told her.

"You don't wanna go get a haircut and put on some real clothes?" she asked him.

It's not that he looked like he "just got out of jail" he just didn't look like Christian Knight. He had on a white tee, some Nike basketball shorts and some Air Force Ones, but something was off. Maybe it was the fact that he didn't have on his hundred thousand dollar watch, Farren couldn't put her finger on it.

"After I eat, we're gonna handle all that," he told her, looking at her, smiling.

Farren decided to let him run the show, which is honestly what he did best, lead. Christian had always been wise beyond his years, she always trusted his judgment. He never steered her wrong in any decisions she made pertaining to her career or her life in general.

Once they got to the restaurant, Christian requested that the two of them be seated in a private room. The hostess didn't understand why or who they thought they were because they weren't celebrities.

Christian asked Farren, "How much money you got on you?"

Her lip curled, "Enough," she told him.

"Give this young hoe a couple hundred dollars, I'm ready to eat. I'm going to the bathroom," he told her.

Farren peeled off two hundred dollars, "Private room please ma'am, now," she told her. See Christian was way nicer than Farren, because it wouldn't even been no money handling, it was mid-day and the restaurant wasn't crowded at all. So the lil girl should have sat them down in the private room like her husband had asked.

When Christian came to the room, he was pleased that Farren had already ordered him a glass of Remy, and there was a chicken Cesar salad waiting on him, with the dressing on the side, as he liked it.

"I see you haven't forgotten some things," he said.

Farren ignored him, "So what's up with you?" she asked.

"We have a few things to do today and tomorrow," he told her.

"I got you. I have to fly to Miami on Friday," she informed him.

"Yeah, we're gon' have to talk about all that," he told her.

"Why can't we talk now?" she questioned.

"Because I want to eat my food in peace," he told her, looking her dead in her eyes. Her heart skipped a beat. Farren hated to admit that she was turned on and scared at the same time.

Christian ordered literally everything on the menu, "Is it good?" she asked, he didn't mumble one word while eating.

He nodded his head and continued eating.

"Have you talked or heard from Greg?" she asked.

Christian's jaw tightened, Farren peeped it real quick. The mentioning of Greg's name triggered something on the inside of him.

He continued eating his food.

"Well, he joined The Cartel," she informed him.

Christian chuckled and shook his head. "You're so clueless. I wish that I could drown your father for being such a selfish bastard by dragging you into that hellhole. The same man who told me to get out while I could years ago, shit so crazy to me," he said.

Farren didn't like his comment, "Chrissy, have some respect."

He banged his hand on the table, the waitress assigned to tend to them quickly exited the private room. "No, you have some respect for me, for yourself, for your children, for your daughter who died in their hands! Don't you forget that Farren! When you're sipping your wine with them fools, don't you forget that," he told her.

Tears sprang out of her eyes, as if a screw in the water faucet was loose. "I know that," she told him.

"Do you really? Because I'm starting to think that you've forgotten," he told her.

"Christian, eat your food. You're pissing me off," she snapped.

"I don't care. You're angry? I'm angry about a lot of shit. I've had my friends turn on me, business partners and a young dumb bitch set me up. So Farren if you're angry, join the motherfucking club," he told her.

She sat back and folder her arms. This nigga was entirely too intense for her.

"And for the record, The Cartel isn't a fan club or a Boy Scout organization. It's not some yoga group for pregnant moms. The Cartel invites you. They seek you for years before you're chosen and even after you're chosen, you have to literally climb up out the mud, kiss their asses for them to invite you in to the Roundtable. It's not what you think it is," he told her.

"There is no way Greg's flashy ass got in The Cartel. I'm not even believing that," he told her.

Farren loved to prove a nigga wrong, it was something she found joy in doing. She shot him her best smile and fished through her purse for her little black book.

Christian watched her. "I don't like your ring," he told her.

"Okay and? Chrissy, I don't care. My days of pleasing you are over," she told him.

"You're not even flashy. Why is it so many diamonds stacked on each other? Whoever did this or whatever local Jewelry store he picked this up from did a horrible job crafting this ring." He observed her wedding ring finger in his hand, carefully examining the ring. He had an eye for the finer things in life; Christian could easily calculate a person's worth up in a few short seconds.

"You're getting on my nerves." Farren rolled her eyes and snatched her hand back.

Farren flipped through her little black book, and searched for her page with notes on Greg. Their meeting did not last long because she did not trust him as a person and definitely wasn't feeling meeting with him, someone she considered family.

Farren slid the notebook over to his side of the table, and watched him read over her notes.

He looked back at her, "Was he at The Roundtable?" he asked.

She nodded her head.

"Did he vote?" he asked.

She nodded her head again.

"He voted yes?" he asked.

Farren motioned his hand with a thumbs down sign and the look on Christian's face crushed her heart, he was visibly hurt.

"What did I do to him?" he asked.

"I don't know Chrissy, he's never called me to check on the kids or nothing. The one time I did call him, he rushed me off the phone and everything," she told him.

"Are you serious?" he asked.

"Dead ass."

"You have an address on him?" he asked.

Farren looked at him, "I can't do that, you know that," she told him.

"I don't remember asking you, let's go," he told her, wiping his mouth and standing to his feet.

She got up after him and waited for him to pay the tab.

"What?" he asked.

"Uh, you done ordered all this food, so you need to pay," she told him.

"You know I don't have any money on me. Damn, I'm not good for a Ruth's Chris meal?" he asked, with a smirk on his face.

"Hell nah, I don't fuck with you," she told him, but left cash on the table to cover his meal and a tip.

"Whatever. Let's go, we got errands to run and I'm not trying to be with you all day," he told her.

She walked in front of him and made her hips sway. "Oh baby, trust me the feeling is mutual," she told him.

Once they got in the car, one of their favorite songs came on the radio. "Christian this used to be our jammmmmmmm," Farren snapped her fingers and turned the radio up.

He rapped the first verse and she sung the chorus, after the song went off.

They both found themselves reminiscing about the good old days. "Man that brought back some memories," he said.

"Remember that time you had me on the bridge for hours while you was with Greg and them?" she asked.

"And you got out the car with your gun ready to kill all of them," he laughed.

Farren was laughing so hard, she had to hold her stomach and drive at the same time.

"Man, I was so scared," she finally admitted, years later.

The car fell silent as the two were both wrapped up in their own thoughts.

Farren wondered where did they lose their magic touch, when did the perfect fairytale come to a conclusion. She was stuck trying to discover the missing pieces of the puzzle. She and Christian were so happy…once…upon…a…time.

Farren turned the radio down, "Can I ask you a question?"

"Shoot," he told her.

"What did I do wrong? What did she have over me?" she finally asked the million dollar question.

He shrugged his shoulders, "She was cool," he said. Three fucking words. Four almost five years later and all she had to say was that she was cool. Cool didn't force you to leave your happy home that came with children and a dog.

Cool didn't have you begging for a divorce, cool didn't leave your wife feeling miserable and embarrassed.

Cool was 'oh she give good head'. Cool was shorty is laidback and from time to time we kick it. Cool is not what got her left. Christian Knight had to come better than that and *cool* was unacceptable.

"Umm, no sir. What else?" she prodded for answers.

"What you want me to say? She was everything you wasn't? Nah, it wasn't none of that. She couldn't cook, she didn't like cleaning, she didn't want kids, and she didn't go to church. You were better than her hands down, but she was cool," he told her.

"Cool? Really. You're knocking on sixty talking about a bitch was cool. What made you say 'damn, I don't want Farren anymore'?" she questioned.

Christian took a deep breath, then went to turn the music back up. Farren slapped his hand.

"Christian, it's unfair for you to not be honest with me," she told him.

"I just wasn't feeling it no more. It wasn't you, it was me," he decided to use the oldest line in the book.

Farren looked over at him and said, "I would hate to leave you on the side of the road."

"Farren, I don't have the perfect answer. Nothing that I can say to you right now can make you feel better, trust me," he told her.

She decided to leave it at that, if he didn't feel like she deserved an explanation then she wouldn't force one out of him.

Farren told herself to let the past be the past. She had been moved on anyway.

"Hey, you still got the condo? I think I wanna just move back in there," he said, once they had got back in the car from stopping to get him a haircut.

"I use the condo often, both Jonte and I do," she told him.

Christian gave her a mean glance. "WOW!" he said loudly.

"Don't start, your other house is waiting for you. I just had someone clean it up," she informed him.

"Good looking out," he said and grabbed her thigh then rubbed it.

"Hmm hmm," she brushed him off.

The two spent the entire day getting Christian's life back in order. Farren gave him the keys to his house and he was impressed that she had kept it up for him over the years, it didn't look or smell dusty. They stopped by the bank so he could reopen his accounts and Farren gladly gave him his money back that she put to the side for him.

Christian asked where his Porsche was, he didn't care about any of the other cars. "Ask your bitch," she told him.

"Damn," he muttered.

Now he had to spend money on a stupid ass car tomorrow. Christian only rode Foreign cars, so he knew he was about to break the bank in the morning.

Farren took Christian to the grocery store and a few stores to get essential things for living. He basically had to get his life together all over again, but she didn't mind helping in the process.

Farren was in the guest bathroom washing her hands. The day had been entirely too long and she was ready to take a much needed bath, she felt sticky.

"What are you doing in here?" she asked.

"Just checking on you" he stated.

"I'm good, always good, been good, and gon' be good," she joked.

Christian rolled his eyes, Farren annoyed him, but right now he needed her. She was his way back in The Cartel to kill a few trifling ass niggas.

Her very existence bothered him, she wasn't the same girl he met so many years ago.

"You look good," he told her, smiling.

Farren dropped her head and started drying her hands with a towel.

"Christian please don't start? I'm over you, okay? Super over you," she told him, quietly.

Christian moved closer to her. "Who are you trying to prove something to, me or you?" he asked.

"Get back," she warned him.

He continued going in her direction, he wanted to be in personal space.

"Why?" he asked.

"I'm not about to fuck you," she told him.

Christian chuckled, "Who said I wanted some pussy?" he asked.

She gave him the "nigga please" look. After being locked up all that time, she was sure he wanted something hot, sticky and tight to slide into, but it would not be her and she meant that.

"When was the last time somebody licked you till you started crying, huh?" Christian finally made his way into Farren's personal space, he wrapped his long arms around her waist and palmed her ass

Somethings hadn't changed and that was Farren soft, round, juicy ass.

"My man just did that the other day," she lied, Farren hadn't let Jonte's cheating ass touch her in weeks.

"That *child* doesn't know how to please you," he told her.

Farren smacked her lips and pushed him away. She was growing tired of Christian and his jokes about Jonte's job, age and finances. She was madly in love with Jonte, and his birth date or account balance didn't measure their love for one another.

Christian was so fucking annoying. They were going to have figure out a way to co-parent because her being around him for a long period of time bothered her.

"You smell so good," he told her, coming up on her again.

"Christian Knight!" she yelled.

He smiled at her. "Farren, stop playing with me," he told her.

She laughed, "I'm not playing with you. I see your dick poking out. I'm not giving you none, you better call Asia. Oops, I forgot. You can't."

Christian eyes went dark, she knew she had entirely too low below the belt. She didn't regret it though, he left her for her and Farren could never forget it.

"When did you start wearing makeup?" he asked.

"It's just eyeliner and mascara, nothing special," she told him.

"Can I kiss you?" he asked.

"No you cannot. Look, I'm getting old. I'm hot, so let me out of here," she moved around him and walked out of the bathroom.

Christian came and swooped her up. "Man, put me down." She tried to punch him.

Christian threw her on the bed and towered over her body and showered her down with kisses and tickled her sides. Farren hadn't been tickled in years. "Oh my God, move! Stop! Chrissy stop!" she couldn't stop laughing.

"I love when you call me that, it does something to me," he stopped and told her.

Farren looked in his eyes and tried to find love in them, but all she was malice. The man she had fell in love with wasn't looking back at her. He reached down and kissed her, and damn…she felt it.

Farren heard the fireworks going off, but it wasn't enough to give him no pussy, nope not at all.

Christian continued kissing her for a few minutes and she allowed him to kiss her in the mouth.

His kisses began to move from her lips, to her neck, to her chest. Christian got up and removed her clothes and Farren allowed him, the room was so silent.

She wasn't even caught up in her thoughts for the first time. Farren just wondered did he even still care. Did he even still love her? She knew that she was over him and it was nothing but the grace of God.

Christian pulled her thong off of her and he took a deep sniff of her panties. "You still smell so sweet," he told her.

She smirked. "Some things don't change," she told him.

Christian took his time, licking the center of her nipples and tugging on them with his tongue and teeth.

Farren allowed her head to fall back in ecstasy. This nigga knew he was the truth with his tongue.

Christian took his time showing her attention. He wanted her to feel comfortable enough to slide up in it.

He thought about getting her pregnant just to piss that nigga Jonte off, but he decided against it as he didn't want any more children.

Christian slowly made his way to one of favorite places. Throughout his life, Christian had traveled to some beautiful places, visited all of the major museums, he was a lover and collectors of rare pieces of art. Christian enjoyed all kinds of food, even the most delicate fish, Christian devoured it all.

But by far, in between Farren's legs still remained one of the most exquisite places he had been to.

She really had a goldmine between her legs. The way that it clenched your tongue, finger and dick, should have been a sport that all women were required to learn in order to keep a man.

The way that it smelled, so pure and clean. Never funky or dirty.

The upkeep of the place was in tip-top shape, never shaved always waxed. No visible bumps or scars.

From this exotic place, his three children came into the world. So when Christian first kissed it, he was paying homage to her; thanking him for making him a father. She gave him the best gift in the world, he was blessed three times.

Farren's place was somewhere that a person could get lost. He sat up using his elbows and took his time, licking and sucking on her most intimate parts.

Christian was trying to smell it all, the fragrance was so inviting. He shoved his head further in there.

Christian damn near nutted when Farren finally decided to let a moan escape from her juicy lips.

Yes! He won. He got her to say his name.

He knew he still had it. "Yes baby, say it again," he came up for air and told her to repeat herself until she came.

Farren couldn't believe this nigga was feeling this good, it was feeling too damn good. She felt the puddle of ecstasy forming from under her.

Christian was pleased to know that she still had it in her, the girl was like a fire hydrant.

And finally…she climaxed.

Farren grabbed her mouth trying to contain her pleasure and satisfaction, but it didn't do anything to silence her. She couldn't help it, that shit felt so good. Christian wiped his mouth and looked up just in time to see her wiping her eyes.

He had achieved his goal.

Farren rolled over on her stomach, trying to catch her breath.

Christian got up quickly and dropped his shorts and boxers, he got back on bed.

Farren turned around real fast and her face scrunched up. "Whoa buddy." She got off the bed and began to search the room for her under garments.

"Really Farren?" Christian asked, ain't this some shit, he was pissed off.

"Christian, you never thought I was about to fuck you? Really?" she asked, with her hands on her hips.

"You just let me eat your pussy and you nutted in my mouth!" he yelled.

"You're welcome for dinner," she told him and finished putting her clothes on.

"Anything else you need before I go?" she asked a few minutes later. Farren was feeling super guilty, but half of her enjoyed it and the other half of her wanted to go find her man so he can finish the job her estranged husband had started.

As good as that head was, Farren had always been a loyal person and her pussy would only be stroked by Jonte. It angered her that she hadn't even heard from her man all day. he hadn't bothered to call or text her today, so she was ready to get alone so she can call and curse his ass out then beg him to fuck her from the back.

"Nah, I'm good. I'm about to get some sleep," he told her. Farren could tell that he had an attitude, but she didn't care. Christian would *never* get her again, ever in his life. He should have thought a little harder about his vows and their marriage before he left her for a stripper bitch.

Farren headed back to his house to drop him off, "Call me in the morning and I'll take you to get your car," he told her.

"Farren, don't forget I need that address."

She ignored him. "I'll hit you later," she told him.

After Christian closed her car door, Farren called Jonte but didn't receive an answer. She already knew where he was, so she did an illegal U-turn in the middle of the road and headed to Hardy.

Farren called her mother. "Ma, is Jonte out there?" she asked.

"Girl, I'm at work. I can't keep up with your nigga and mine," she told her.

"Alright bye," she said and disconnected the call, her mama could never just say yes or no, she always had something slick to say. It irritated Farren when her mama did that, but unbeknownst to Farren, she did the same thing.

Farren made her way to Hardy and she silently prayed that she didn't have to act a fool out here in the Courtyard today. Her kids were in Atlanta visiting Ashley, so no bitch would be spared today.

Farren drove around the complex a few times looking for her fiancé's car and couldn't find it, she wondered where he was. She knew he wasn't at the restaurant and probably wasn't at home. Where in the hell was he?

Farren parked her car and tapped her fingers on her steering wheel, racking her brain trying to see where this dude was. His condo! As soon as the thought came to her mind, she went to reverse her car and head in that direction when the dirty son of a bitch pulled in next to her with the hoe in his car.

Jonte was so caught up in the moment that he didn't even notice Farren was parked next to him.

He got out of the car and so did she, with a bag of Popeye's in her hand and a large soda. Farren rolled her eyes, Jonte was not getting the hint, and apparently her threats were going in one ear and out the other.

Farren contemplated on showing her ass or going home and going to bed because she was super sleepy. She decided to go home, she was entirely too old to be in the hood arguing with a woman over her supposed to be man, plus she had just received some mind-blowing head and was sleepy. In Farren's eyes, Jonte was the one to blame, he was the stepping out and lying. Farren wasn't in a relationship with Trina, she was in one with Jonte.

She knew that Jonte was only acting out, because of her recent activity with The Cartel, but that was still no excuse to be disrespectful. At the current point in Farren's life, she was unconcerned with keeping up after a man.

Once she made it home, she told herself that would be the last time she popped up on his ass, what's done in the dark eventually always comes to the light, and Jonte ass was playing in the sun.

After fixing her a glass of wine, she sat in bed and caught up on some much needed reading, Farren decided to go on and go to Miami. She couldn't ignore Bianchi's ass forever, sooner or later he would be coming to look for her ass and Farren damn sure didn't want trouble at her doorstep. Her home was her safe haven and where her children laid their head, she didn't want any problems with him. Farren couldn't believe that she allowed Christian to taste her again, the feeling came back and she clenched her legs tight together trying to erase the memories out of her head.

She had to stay out of his way. Christian was on a mission to get her back, or so she thought.

In all honesty, Christian just wanted some pussy, he really wasn't stunting Farren. She was cool and all, but their time together had come to an end a very long time ago.

*****

Christian

Christian slept peacefully in his new home. He was grateful that Farren had kept the home in decency and in order, he was worried that he would be released and came to nothing. Although Christian had done Farren horrible in the past, the fact still remained that they were for one, still married and secondly, at one point in life they were madly in love. Despite, how her family and the few friends she did have felt about Christian, one thing no one could ever deny was that Christian was a great provider. It was only right that Farren gave him his money back that she took from his personal banker a few years ago. Christian just knew that she blew through all his earnings, but she had her own money.

Christian came home on a personal mission to destroy some motherfuckers. He was done with the game for sure, but blood would be shed before he bowed out gracefully.

He couldn't believe that last night, he ate Farren's pussy, he just knew that they were going to fuck all night and until the sun came up for old time's sake, but Farren proved him wrong.

She really loved that ole broke ass nigga, but hey, to each its own.

Christian finally opened his eyes after an extensive amount of hours of rest. He was ready to get his day started because he had a lot to do.

He sat up in bed and his heart jumped out of his chest. He reached under his pillow for his gun and it was gone.

How the fuck did this nigga get in his house? He couldn't believe less than twenty-fours after he had been released he had been caught slipping.

"Aww man come on now, you know me better than that," Greg said.

"What's up?" Christian asked.

"Chris, how was it in there?" he asked.

"Go on and kill me cus I don't have two words to say to you," he told him.

"Well, I wanna talk first," Greg told him.

"Matter of fact, let me go find a chair around this big ass house. This shit is nice too. Farren did her thing," Greg said with a smirk on her face.

Greg turned around and left the room.

Christian didn't even have the strength to fight this nigga. He hadn't a chance to get a cell phone yet, and the house phone was downstairs in the kitchen.

He did get up and put on some pajama pants and lit a blunt.

"Okay, I'm back," Greg took a deep breath and sat down with not one but two guns on his lap.

"Greg, what's up with you, man?" Christian asked. He thought about playing mind games, but this nigga wasn't dumb at all.

"Nigga, you can't tell me you wasn't gunning for me. Come on now Chrissy, I can't even believe it," he joked.

"Greg, what did I ever do to you? That's my only question," he asked.

"What did you do? What did you not do? You ain't do shit. You wasn't the real Connect, homey. That was me, I put that work in!" he yelled him.

Christian dropped his head. Damn, it's always the nigga you least expect to cross you. Best friend since the 6th grade, Godfather to all three of his children, best man in his wedding, pallbearer at his daddy's funeral, the only nigga who knew the code to his safe. Christian really couldn't believe it. Despite what so many people thought, he handled his business well as the Connect.

Greg must have been having amnesia. It was *Christian Knight* who got the plug, *Christian Knight*, who used to take those long trips down the highway, *Christian Knight*, who put the first hundred thousand up for them to cop. It was *Christian Knight's wit* and charm that got the overseas accounts set up. *Christian Knight's money* that kept the lights on in the trap houses. *Christian Knight* may have not been in the trenches with the .44 on his lap, but better believe *Christian Knight* paved the way for niggas to ride in the car to get to the trenches, provided money to buy the .44 and the bullets and silencer. *Christian Knight* played his position as the *Connect* very well, he did what he had to do and that was to lead and execute orders.

Now whatever issue Greg may had been having could have been discussed years ago, but either way it goes, at the end of the day, it was *Christian Knight* whose name was linked to everything that this selfish, jealous motherfucker ever had.

Christian laughed. "Let me guess, Kiss was your cousin. You put him on to me, had Asia fall in love with me, you let her rat me out, then you turned your back on Kiss and killed him. You know what's crazy my brother? Asia never fucking liked you and on so many occasions she wanted to tell me something…I felt it when she would talk to me, something wasn't right. Greg, you deserve a round of applause." Christian clapped his hands.

Greg looked surprised. Christian continued, "See, I have always been a busy man being the Connect and all, so while incarcerated, I was able to think. I took myself back to a conversation we had when you wanted to start moving the weight in jail with your cousin…a young nigga named Kiss and I kept saying nah I'm not feeling that and you was getting mad because I didn't let you get your way as your bitch ass normally did," he said.

Greg spoke up, "Let me clear this up you, since you think you figured it out. My cousin is still living for one, I'm not no pussy ass nigga. He got his half and we went our separate ways. That bitch Asia had no problem setting you up, sorry to burst your bubble. I'm about to kill your ass because I don't fuck with you and you're not about to come back to take my spot at the Roundtable." He waved his gun around.

"That's why you didn't vote for me?" Christian shook his head.

"See, if Farren stays out of my way, I'll stay out of hers. Make sure to send her a signal from heaven," Greg told him.

"If you…" Before he could finish his sentence, Greg sent one straight to his head, "zip" the silencer let out a little noise.

Greg just killed his best friend and didn't feel not one ounce of regret.

Matter of fact he was proud of himself. He just murdered the mother fucking *Connect*.

Rest in Peace Christian Knight.

Chapter Three

Farren

"Are you okay?" Ashley asked Farren. She had been staring at the wall in the dressing room for a few minutes.

"Farren," Ashley called her name again.

"I hear…you. I hear you okay? Do not yell at me," she managed to get out. Talking was a hassle, along with eating, sleeping, smiling, anything that required her to think or move a muscle, was difficult for Farren to do.

Six days ago, she walked into her estranged husband's house and found him dead. Dead. Christian Knight had died. Someone had the balls to kill Christian Knight.

Farren sat in her throw up for hours, unable to move.

She couldn't breathe, she couldn't cry. She stared. She stared at his lifeless body and wondered how in the hell did this happen and who the fuck did it.

Oh but Farren knew, she knew who did it and as soon as she got her mind together she was going to murder that sneaky motherfucker.

But for now, she sat stagnant in the dressing room.

"Farren try this on," Ashley went to pull Farren's shirt off and saw speckles of blood in Farren's fingernails.

"Farren is this…" she started to say, blood.

Farren put her finger over Ashley's mouth and she almost gagged at the horrid smell.

"Don't say his name, don't you dare say it," she told her with big eyes and tears rolling down her face.

Ashley peeled her finger away and placed two hands on Farren's shoulders. "Sister, who I love so much. You have to pull it together. Your children need you," she told her.

Farren broke down to the floor, her howling could be heard throughout Dillard's. No one knew what was going on, but if they knew heartbreak and heartache, they would know that those tears were of a woman who was dealing with death, dealing with their life ending, dealing with not being able to mutter true feelings because she assumed that she always had time, always had just one more day to get it right.

Farren couldn't believe this had happened to her, she didn't want to believe that tomorrow she was burying her husband. Although she had moved on and had given birth to another's man child, she considered herself a widow. Farren didn't think they would end this way.

She had so much more to say to him, so many more questions to ask. Christian had literally been her rock and her world for many, many years. He'd groomed her into the wife that he had prayed for. Farren owed so much to Christian, and she never really got to tell him thank you.

Her tears finally dried and she got herself together, not all the way, but enough to walk out of the department store and go home and crawl in bed.

Farren couldn't think straight, she just remembered waking up the next morning and looking extra cute. Jonte had crawled his no-good, lying cheating ass into bed in the wee hours of the morning, but she was too tipsy to care. She rolled over on him and pretended to be asleep. When he fell asleep and started snoring that was when she turned her lamp light on and went back to journaling.

Farren woke up the next day with a smile on her face. She sung all of her and Christian's favorite songs in the shower. She even wore white, which was his favorite color.

She stopped at Dunkin Donuts, got him a coffee and two doughnuts. She copped a cellphone, since he didn't get a chance to cop him one the previous day.

Today they were getting him a car then were going to fly to Atlanta together to get the kids. That was the plan she had construed the night before. She knew Christian would say yes because he wanted to redeem himself as a father.

Farren hummed to herself as she patiently waited for him to come to the door, Christian had never been a late sleeper, always up before dawn. After about five minutes of ringing the door bell and knocking profusely, she went and got her key out of her car and unlocked the front door.

Farren called out his name, "Chrissy!" She turned the television in the living room off.

"Chrissy, I know you not still sleeping nigga," she said loudly.

Farren made her way to his bedroom and OH MY GOD the sight before her was a bloody massacre, it was a mess.

Who the fuck killed Christian Knight? Farren didn't even cry, she didn't feel not one tear roll down her face. She was hurt, she was so hurt. She felt like someone came and knocked the wind right out of her. This was not how the story was supposed to end, he wasn't even able to tuck his kids in one last time, see Noel off to prom or her wedding, nor witness Michael graduate. He didn't even get a chance to kiss his mother's cheek...Like wow, this was totally unfair.

Farren threw up from the smell, she didn't even bother to wipe it up. Her body continued to twitch from shock.

She stood there and was unable to process that he had died. She wondered how long he laid there without life in his body; someone came and stole his soul.

Her phone vibrating in her hand brought her back to reality, it was JONTE.

She slid the bar across to answer, but words wouldn't come out. She tried to speak, but couldn't.

Jonte constantly said hello.

Finally her brain told her to speak.

"Dead...he's dead...he's dead. He's dead, Chrissy is dead," she cried.

The line went silent. "Where are you?" he asked.

"His old house, I came to get him to go get him a car and a cellphone. He got shot...shot in the head. He's dead. Christian is dead," she cried some more.

"Baby, call the police and go sit in your car. Don't touch anything," he told her.

"Send me your location?" Jonte asked. Thank God for updated technology, Farren was entirely too distraught to be typing anything. A few clicks and touches and her location was sent right to his phone.

Jonte hopped out the bed and didn't even bother showering. He threw last night's clothes back on and went to be there for his girl.

Farren made the 911 call and went and sat in the living room. Of course the police arrived immediately, but she was still in shock.

Jonte tried to get into the house, but it had officially been marked off as a crime scene investigation.

Farren heard him outside getting rowdy and snapped out of it. She opened the front door, went under the yellow caution tape and ran into his arms. Jonte didn't care that she was covered in throw up he held her tight.

Farren was completely lost. She was confused and all she could think about was GREG. She was gone get his ass. He robbed a man of his home, his family, and his children.

Farren's mind went to Bianchi and wondered if it was him. Whoever it was would be getting theirs real soon.

"I wanna take you home," Jonte told her after she had been cleared at the police station.

"I got so many calls to make. I need to call his sister, his niece...damn, that's really it. Christian lost all his friends when he went away," she mumbled sadly.

"Baby, I'll do that, come on," he told her, helping her to her feet. Farren was extremely weak.

At this time, she didn't care that she had just caught him with another female, Farren just needed to be held, she needed to hear him say that everything was going to be okay.

The entire ride he never said anything, he did hold her hand and rubbed it and every few minutes he looked over at her to make sure she was okay, knowing she wasn't.

Christian Knight died. No matter how many times she said it, it still didn't process.

Once they pulled up at home, Farren sat in the car unable to move. Ashley turned the engine off. "Farren, do you think you're able to go to the funeral?" she hesitated before asking, but she really didn't think it was best for her to go.

Farren was mentally unstable. She wanted to drop a sedative in her wine, just so she could get some sleep.

Farren never looked her way. With her oversized Chloe sunglasses perched on her nose, she didn't respond to her best friend. She got out the car and went into her home.

Her children were all in the living room watching a movie with Jonte. Farren didn't bother to speak, she went straight to her bedroom.

Jonte shook his head, but didn't say anything because the kids were present. They didn't care that their mom didn't speak, they were too busy trying to see what was about to happen next.

When Jonte broke the news to the kids, Farren just stood at the door of Noel's room with her head against the wall and her arms crossed.

Noel didn't cry, she just said that she would pray he made it to heaven with Carren. She loved Jonte and had it been him that was taken away she would have a fit. Whereas Michael punched the wall and threw shit all over his room. Jonte let him hash it out because he was really going through it and he knew what it felt like to lose someone really close to you. Jonte missed his brother every single day.

Ashley came into the house. "Jonte, can I speak with you in the kitchen for a second?" she asked.

Jonte removed a sleeping Morgan from his lap and laid her down on the couch, then covered her with a blanket and kissed her forehead. He loved his little munchkin.

"I am extremely worried about Farren. Even with Dice she didn't act like this, she looks like she's' about to die any second," she told her best friend's fiancé.

"If she does that, then she's selfish as hell and not thinking about her kids," he told her straight up. Jonte was allowing Farren her space to grieve and mourn because he knew how much Christian Knight really meant to her, but eventually she was going to have to snap out of it, seriously.

"I don't know what to do," Ashley said, sounding defeated.

"I'm about to go check on her. She barely talks to me, maybe today will be different," he said.

Jonte took a deep breath before he entered the room, a loud ass breath Farren heard him breathing before he opened the door to their master bedroom.

"How are you feeling?" he asked, laying in the bed next to her.

He saw that she had put her wedding ring back on and took off her engagement ring; a sign of ultimate disrespect.

He said nothing.

"I don't know," she whispered, he could barely hear her.

"After tomorrow this will all be over, we can go on vacation," he told her, rubbing her arm.

Farren jerked away. "Is Trina going with us?" she asked, allowing the cold to drip from her voice.

Farren wanted to hate Jonte so she wouldn't feel so bad about missing Christian.

"I just came to check on you, I'm going back to the front," he told her and got out the bed.

"Farren?" Jonte called her name out.

She didn't respond but he knew that she heard his ass.

"Tomorrow at the burial, you need to drop that ring in the ground with him and put the one that I bought for you back on, or I'm leaving you. I'm not playing sideline to a nigga that's dead," he said and closed the bedroom door.

Farren sat up in that bed so fast, she couldn't believe he checked her.

Jonte was being very rude and disrespectful.

She heard her cell phone ringing, but she didn't move a muscle to answer it. She didn't like talking. Talking was a struggle for her.

Her phone had been ringing off the hook with people calling, she never answered the phone, not for one person.

Even her mother couldn't get her on the line nor her sister. Kim, who had become a good friend of hers, had been trying for days but Farren couldn't talk.

The last person she had a conversation was with Christian Knight.

The last person who made her smile was Christian Knight, the last person who she had kissed, who kissed her, made her cum, made her laugh, sung a song with, had ice cream with was Christian Knight.

Things ended too soon and she just prayed that God softened her heart and mended it all the same time.

She was hurting and felt herself breaking down slowly but surely.

Farren already knew Bianchi was going to be pulling her to the side tomorrow. She had yet to go see him and had blocked his and Jeff's number from her phone. Mario texted her the other day and he was one of the lucky ones that got a simple one word text back saying, "thank you" she couldn't manage to type much, but she did tell him thank you for checking up on her.

Farren wanted to be there to comfort Chloe and the rest of the family, but she couldn't. She was barely comforting her damn self, let alone being able to offer her condolences to someone else.

She tried to fall asleep, but couldn't. All she saw was blood, his blood everywhere.

She wondered who went back and cleaned all that blood up.

Farren closed her eyes again but popped them right back up, when she saw that his eyes were wide open staring back at her. She wondered what his last words were.

Farren got out of bed and fell to her knees to pray.

Ashley rushed in the room, "Are you okay? I was headed to the laundry room and I heard the thump," she said.

Farren laughed, whew...she finally laughed.

Ashely looked at her silly, this bitch was really losing it, she thought to herself.

"I was about to pray," she told her.

"Oh...okay. Well pray, you need it," she told her.

"Can you pray with me?" she asked her best friend.

Ashley put the wicker basket down by the foot of the bed and joined her best friend on her knees, she held her hand.

"God please send me a sign or a wonder of what to do and what to think, even how to feel. Soften my heart, open my eyes and ears. God whatever you want me to do, I will do it. Please send me peace. Amen," she whispered.

"Farren, I know you're sad about Christian, but did something happen before he died because last time I checked you hated him or was it a front?" she asked.

Farren shook her head, she never bothered to say anything, never even offered an explanation. She always believed in privacy and she didn't feel the need to prove a point or to make Ashley understand why she was feeling the same way.

It wasn't the head that had Farren tripping, it was after all of the bullshit, all of the madness, tears, pulling the gun on him, Carren's death, the abortions and various trips to the clinics. That one day they spent together was everything, it was as if they had never fell off before. Those precious moments would be near and dear to Farren's heart for a very, very long time to come. Christian Knight had left a staple on her heart, she had a serious weak spot for him.

Men like Christian Knight were considered a woman's dream come true. Christian Knight, was tall, charming, sexy, intelligent, well-rounded and well-dressed. Christian Knight spoke so many different languages, he had traveled the world more than twice. Christian Knight never apologized for not being ghetto or a thug, he had thanked his mother constantly for her good home training along with his daddy for teaching him manners and the importance of saving his money. Christian Knight didn't like partying, but don't get it twisted that nigga loved him the strip club. Oh the irony of him allowing him a stripper bitch to be his downfall.

Christian Knight enjoyed life to the fullest and he considered Farren Knight the perfect wife. She was amazing, it was sad that he didn't get to tell her how much he really did love and appreciate her before he passed. Farren just needed some closure, confirmation and clarification for her feelings. She really didn't know how to feel right now.

"I'm about to take a nap. Are the kids' clothes together?" she asked.

Ashley promised her that tomorrow would be a breeze, the kids would be taken care of and all she had to do was get dressed so they can make it to the funeral on time.

Once Ashley left the bedroom, Farren laid her head down on her pillows. She was sad, but she knew she had to get it together real soon, she couldn't go on with life this way. Six days ago her life did a 180, but after tomorrow she had to get back to business. Christian Knight wouldn't want her wallowing in her misery.

Farren was so tired of her damn phones ringing, she threw her business phone at the wall.

"Thump!" it fell to the floor.

But that wasn't the one that was ringing and vibrating off the hook, it was her personal line.

"HELLO. HELLO. HELLO!" she answered the phone in frustration. Whoever the fuck it was, was about to receive the wrath of Farren.

"Damn man, what's going on with you?" Kool's voice instantly softened her.

She took a deep breath, "Tired of my phone ringing," she told him.

"How are you?" he asked.

"Tired. What time is it?" she asked.

"It's still early, not even midnight," he said.

"You're here for the fu...funeral?" it was so hard for her to say the word funeral. Funeral meant that Christian had died, he had really died and that was something that she was unable to accept at this time.

"Yeah, to show my respect," he told her.

"I thought you didn't like New York?" she asked.

"I don't, no real niggas up here," Kool told her, she could tell that he was smoking.

"Where are you staying?" she asked him.

"JW Marriott."

"Do you have company?" she questioned.

"You're so nosey shawty. Nah, I'm solo dolo as always," he told her.

"I'm on the way, send me your room number," she told him.

"Alright."

"Aye!" Kool called out.

"Bring me some chicken, I'm high as hell," he said.

Farren laughed, it felt good to laugh. "I got you."

She didn't want to bathe, but she knew she needed to.

She didn't want his smell to leave her body, she wanted him to stay on her forever. Farren had been taking bird baths for a week, which is not like her, she prided herself on bathing three or four times a day, in her personal opinion cleanliness was next to Godliness.

She turned the water on steaming hot, then went to adjust it to a temperature she was comfortable with, Farren peeled the clothes off of her body, and stepped into the shower.

She stood there, holding her stomach remembering when she first told Christian she was pregnant.

He was so happy.

Farren bathed quietly, humming their wedding song under her breath. *Here &*
Now by Luther Vandross was there song and it was one of their favorite songs to sing
together.

She would be okay, God had always healed her.

She stepped out of the shower, feeling like a new person. Her hair was soak and
wet but she didn't care, she French braided it back and applied lotion to her body,
throwing on leggings, a Victoria Secret pullover and her black Nike flip-flops.

She grabbed her purse, phone and keys off of the floor.

Farren hadn't drove in a few days, Jonte felt like she wasn't in her right mind to
be driving.

She bypassed him sitting at the bar in the kitchen table rolling a blunt. "Where
you going?"

"I'll be back," she told him.

"I asked you a question," he stated.

"Do you question Trina like that? Huh? Do you keep tabs on her?" she asked.

"Bye Farren," he said and turned back around to tend to what he was doing prior
to her thinking she was slick trying to sneak out the house.

But the thing was, Farren wasn't sneaking, Jonte didn't sneak around doing the
trifling shit he did, so she wasn't either.

Besides, her and Kool were nothing and wouldn't be nothing. She just wanted to
be in an unfamiliar setting.

Farren stopped and got him a box of chicken from this local hood spot, she loved
their food, along with some potato wedges and baked beans.

Farren went to the Arab store and got a bottle of wine because she knew Kool's
ghetto ass didn't have any wine in his hotel room.

She called him once she made it outside his door. She didn't want to know in fear
of other members of The Cartel staying at this hotel, and she didn't need none of these
niggas in her business.

"Why you just didn't knock?" he asked.

"Why do you have your gun out?" she asked.

"Bad habit, don't' take it personal," he told her.

Farren was a lil hesitant before walking in, this nigga was coo-coo.

"Man, come on," he told her, grabbing the food her hands. Farren stepped inside of the hotel room.

"You look horrible," he observed.

Farren popped the cork on the wine bottle and poured her a glass.

"I'll look like a million bucks tomorrow, trust me," she told him, winking her eye.

Kool dived in on the food, he started tearing it up.

"This chicken good as hell, appreciate it," he said.

"Mmm hmm." She got comfortable on the couch.

"How long will you be here?" she asked.

"Leaving right after the funeral, got shit to handle back home," he informed her.

"I'm ready to get back to work" Farren needed something to occupy her mind.

"Man that shit is crazy how it happened. How you get knocked the day you get out of jail? Somebody was waiting on his ass," he said.

Farren remained silent, she continued to sip her wind. She knew Greg did it.

"Tell me what's on your mind?" he requested.

"I'm just trying to see am I bad luck. My first love died in front of me, Christian comes home and the next morning he gets shot…What is it about me?" she finally admitted.

How come love never stayed with her long? It was like nothing lasted forever. Farren didn't know if she was happy that Jonte was fucking around on her, so she could use it as leverage to stay from around him. She didn't want anything to happen to him on the strength of her. A lot of people depended on Jonte to eat, he couldn't dare leave this earth before his time.

"Don't think like that, shit happens in life. It's life baby girl, good days are not promised," he preached to her.

"Christian had me feeling something that I hadn't felt in a very, very long time, and I…I don't know how to feel. I'm confused," she told him.

"I thought y'all had broken up?" he asked.

"We did. We are. It's been over, but I don't know… I just don't think that I was all the way done. Like in the back of my mind, I think that I still loved him."

"Love makes women weak." He shook his head and took a puff on his blunt.

"Uh and niggas too," she told him.

Kool shook his head. "Not me. I ain't falling in love no time soon, it's not for me. I'm stacking my bread and staying out of the way."

"You don't have kids?" she asked.

"Nope and I don't want none. I got tons of bad ass nieces and nephews," he said.

"So you're telling me that you don't have a main bitch?" Farren couldn't believe him at all.

Kool shook his head, "Ma, you're not hearing me are you? I'm good on that."

"So when you travel, who do you go out of town with?"

"If I'm not making a run, I'm not traveling. I don't spend unnecessary money on bullshit," he told her.

"Why not enjoy life though? You only live once."

"Farren, I'm under the radar. I've got a one bedroom condo that I fuck bitches in and I got a lil house out west, my house is laid because that's where I spend the majority of my time. I don't like going out because I don't like crowds. If I'm at the booty club, I got a private section. I don't drink because I don't like how alcohol makes me feel. I'm not having any kids because my freedom isn't promised and it's selfish for me to bring kids in this world knowing I'm in the streets. And I'm not falling in love because I trust no one. So in the end, it's just me. I got me all day every day," he told her.

"Your dick must be small?" she asked. What he said was real talk, but at the end of the day, this nigga couldn't convince her that he didn't want a woman to lay beside at night or when it was raining.

Kool was tricking off on somebody, she wasn't with the bullshit.

"I'll let you find out," he told her and hit the blunt.

"Ha!" she joked.

He was cool, his vibe reminded her of Dice.

"I need to be making my way home." She stood to her feet, she had been gone for about an hour and Jonte had a way of finding her every single time.

"You be strong tomorrow." He walked her to the hotel door from the living room area in the hotel suite.

"I'll try my hardest," she told him.

Kool gave her a long hug and she exhaled, needing to just let go and breathe for a moment.

"You're gonna be alright," he promised her.

Kool gave her a lil kiss on her forehead.

"Let me know when you make it home," he told her. Farren walked back to her car super confused. What in the hell was going on and what just happened? She felt a little something, she had to keep it real herself.

In all honesty, her feeling was all over the place. Farren didn't know how or what to feel about anything.

She made it back home and Jonte was in the living room, Farren didn't speak when she entered the house and neither did he.

For the first time in what felt like forever, she was able to sleep.

The next morning was surprisingly peaceful, Farren told the kids in the limo ride over to the church that is was Christian's way of saying that he had made it home with Carren.

Jonte couldn't stop staring at his fiancée, she looked drop-dead gorgeous. In a matter of three hours, Farren's glam squad had brought her back to life. She looked good enough to eat, the tailor-made Dior pantsuit she wore fit her body to a T, and her tall slender frame did the suit no justice. Her hair was freshly pressed and although she bore no makeup, the fresh facial she had received this morning removed the look of sadness and sleepless nights.

Farren looked beautiful. However, as good as she looked that gloomy feeling still loomed over her. She sat staring out of the window, praying that this day would be rushed.

Noel held her mother's hand, she looked just as sad as she did when her sister died.

"Mommy, how did you and daddy meet?" Noel asked.

Farren smiled and Ashley remembered the day Farren called to tell her that she had decided to talk to someone and move on from Dice. Ashley could never forget the fear that was in Farren's voice, the worry and anxiety she was feeling. Farren never wanted to replace Dice. He was so special to her, but men like Christian Knight didn't come around twice, so she knew she had to get him.

"At the mall. Daddy had come into the mall to return some shoes and it was on ever since then," she told her daughter.

"Are you sad?" Morgan asked.

Farren looked at Jonte, who waited for an answer.

"Yes baby, I'm very sad," she said. Farren took a deep breath as the limo came to a complete stop, Jonte stopped out first making sure the kids had got out safely. Ashley told her best friend, "Sis you got this"

Farren was greeted by her mother and sister and even Diane flew in and for that Farren was grateful. Everyone was stopping her, offering her condolences and kissing her cheek.

Farren saw Kool and he saw her too, they didn't too much though, knowing a million and one eyes were staring in her direction. Farren hugged Christian's mother, it had been extremely too long since she last seen her, and she made a mental note to stop by and see her often. Mrs. Knight was a very important part of her life, transitioning from a lost girl. Even though she was grown when Christian decided to court her, he had still turned her into a woman.

Farren didn't make eye contact with anyone from The Cartel, and she knew she better had not seen Greg's lying vindictive ass anywhere in sight. Farren came to the funeral strapped and it was nothing for her to pull her gun out and kill him on sight. She wanted his blood, point, blank period.

Farren took her seat on the front row, with her children sitting on both sides of her, as the Pastor began the funeral, Farren wiped a lone tear from her eye.

She didn't want Christian's body present only because in her personal opinion he didn't like the same boss ass nigga he was before he was sent away. Farren wanted everyone to remember Christian Knight, for being the suave, calm and smooth gentlemen he always was.

Christian Knight had changed Farren's life around in more ways than one. After the death of her beloved Dice, she just knew she would be alone forever and in came Christian Knight showing her a whole new way to love. Yes, he was amazing in bed, but it was the talks that they had, the lessons he taught her, their arguments and most importantly, their separation that strengthened her as a woman. Farren knew what she could and wouldn't accept from a man after dealing with Christian Knight. He took her through a plethora of emotions over the years, but the one that she would say stood out from the most was, unpredictable.

Christian Knight would wake up and say, "We're going to Paris, I have a taste for their wine." He was always doing something new, trying something new, traveling to exotic places, eating exquisite food, getting Farren out of the bed at four in the morning to dance to some old school cd he came across looking for a file for work. Farren had made so many wonderful memories with her husband by her side.

Farren couldn't believe that she was burying her husband. Her spirit must have left her body and went to Heaven with Christian because if someone was to ask Farren how was the funeral she wouldn't be able to say anything because she didn't know. Farren just sat there thinking about the good times. Now that he wasn't here anymore, the good days damn sure outweighed the bad days.

Farren remembered one day they were preparing to visit Egypt for the first time…

Farren knocked on Christian's door before she entered his office.

"Come in bae," he called out.

Christian still had on his business attire from this morning, the time was now ten p.m. He had been at the office all day working tirelessly only to come home to make sure that his responsibilities as the Connect were taken care of as well.

Being that both incomes were equally important to him, he made sure that all of his affairs were in order before they were to travel for eight days for a much-needed vacation.

"What do you need me to pack for you, baby?" she asked.

Farren always knocked and waited until he said the she could come in. As his wife, she was very respectful of his privacy. Farren didn't go looking for dirt, she didn't ask questions she knew she couldn't handle the answer to. Farren allowed Christian to be the man of their household, she didn't bother him. Christian appreciated his wife, she was graceful and very calm. Farren was everything he had always prayed for in a wife.

"Hi baby, come here. How was your day?" he reached out to her. Farren smiled and went and sat in his lap.

"Chrissy, we leave in the morning and you aren't packed yet," she complained.

"Why are we even packing? Let's just buy everything when we get there," he told her with a big smile.

"No baby, we need to pack. I just went and bought these custom pieces to wear at night when we're in the desert," she told him.

"Baby, no leave that stuff here. It's a few places I wanna take you to shop," he told her.

Christian liked seeing Farren in certain colors, especially white. Farren looked like an Arabic queen when she had that all white on especially when her diamonds were draping from her ears and necks, he loved it.

"Chrissy, how was your day?" she asked.

"Long as hell, I need a drink and some head," he said, leaning back with his eyes closed.

It didn't take Farren long to tend to her husband's requests. She got up and fixed him a cup of Remy and dropped to her knees and sucked the stress out of him.

About fifteen minutes later, she was wiping her mouth and brushing her teeth in their guest bathroom and kissing Christian on the cheek.

"I'm going to bed. Love you, baby" she told him.

"Night boo," he told her, patting her ass before she walked off and closed his office door.

Christian loved how Farren always catered to his every need, he had him a certified lady on his team and he couldn't wait to bless her once they got overseas.

Farren chuckled loudly and her children looked over at her, wondering what was so funny about Auntie Chloe talking over the microphone about their father.

Truth be told, Farren wasn't stunting Chloe's fake lying ass. She got lost the entire funeral thinking about her and Christian.

The funeral wasn't long and for that she was extremely thankful, what was long and draining was all of the people coming to speak.

Once Mr. Bianchi made his way to her, her body tensed up and Jonte felt it because he was standing directly right behind her.

"Mr. Bianchi, thank you for coming," she told him through a forced smile.

"Farren, I need to see you this week. My patience has ran thin," he told her and walked off.

She looked back at Jonte and rolled her eyes, she was so over the Cartel and their bullshit.

Farren went and hugged Kennedy and Christian's family one more time, before it was time to say goodbye.

"I'm here if y'all ever need anything," she told the family.

Chloe spoke up, "I'll be calling you sometime next week, so we can take your name off of his accounts and stuff."

Farren tuned back around, "Excuse me?"

"Farren, today has been peaceful, now don't start with me. We just want my brother's money that's all. Don't make this bigger then what it has to be," she said.

"Take me to court boo," Farren told her and walked off.

The nerve of that selfish bitch. When Christian first was sent away it was Farren that made sure they had money put up. It wasn't that she was trying to keep his money hostage, but was Chloe for real? As if Farren wasn't raising two of his children. It was sad that her mind was already on money, it hadn't even crossed Farren's mind.

An hour later, Farren dropped a single white rose in Christian's grave and her wedding ring in there too, she kept her band because it was entirely too sentimental to her.

"Chrissy, I loved you so much. I really did," she whispered before walking away.

She would always miss Christian Knight, always and forever and death really did separate them.

Farren finally made her way back to the limo, where her family had been patiently waiting on her to say her goodbyes.

"I'm hungry, Farren what do you have a taste for?" Ashley asked.

"Nothing really, I'm probably about to pack a bag and fly out to Miami," she said looking out the window.

"You're leaving again?" Noel asked, sadly.

"Yes, but I'll be back tomorrow. Mommy has a meeting baby," she told her daughter.

Jonte shook his head but said nothing, Farren's priorities was so fucked up in his opinion.

The limousine brought them back home and Ashley took the kids to dinner and a movie in an attempt to keep their spirits lifted considering they buried their father today.

Farren moseyed around the house, cleaning up and getting things in order before she left.

Jonte sat at the bar watching her move around him as if he wasn't even there, "You're still not talking to me?" he finally asked.

"What would you like me to say to you, sweetie?" she asked him sarcastically.

"I want my fiancée back," he told her.

Farren giggled. "Fiancée? I knew that I had to tell you something. There will be no wedding, none of that. I'm good," she told him.

Jonte's face turned red. "What the fuck you mean you're good?" he asked.

"I'm not marrying again and I'm damn sure not marrying a nigga who can't keep his dick in his pants. I do not condone cheating. I keep telling you that over and over again and over and over again, yet I keep catching you with this bitch Trina. It's super disrespectful and I'm not going to marry your ass, period," she told him.

"I don't see what's wrong with having an open relationship," Jonte told her as if that shit was going to be acceptable.

"You can't be serious right now? Are you serious? Really?" she asked.

"Ma, you know I love you and you know I care. You know you're my world and my everything. She doesn't mean anything to me, but I fuck with her cus she's cool. Why does that bother you if I'm being honest about it?"

Farren couldn't do anything but sit back and stare. A few years later and this is what they had come to? This dumb ass nigga was pleading for an open relationship.

Farren chose Jonte despite what she heard, no one ever denied that he was a real ass nigga. The issue was that he made stupid decisions and acted on impulse. Jonte could never stay out of jail long enough to reap the benefits of his hard work. But with Farren in his corner, he had been walking the straight and narrow. This hoe, Trina, was ratchet. She didn't care about his future or his children. She thought sitting in Hardy and smacking on boiled peanuts was cute. She thought rolling his blunts for him and counting a few thousand dollars for him proved her loyalty. Trina wasn't a real bitch and she didn't have real bitch tendencies, she didn't encourage him to go legit and work on his credit. Didn't make sure he went to the dentist and doctor regularly, didn't get on her knees and pray for his safety when he was out doing God knows what. Farren did.

And Jonte had the nerve to ask for an open relationship with a girl that was nowhere near her league. You wanna invite another bitch in, at least let it be a woman and not some young girl. Let it be somebody with some ambition and something going on for themselves.

Farren looked over at Jonte with pure disgust. "I'm going to walk away now, I want you to think about what the fuck you just said to me," she told him and left him in the kitchen with his thoughts.

The next morning, Farren and Ashley told the children goodbye as they both made their way to the airport. Farren was headed to Miami to meet with Mr. Bianchi before he came looking for her and Ashley was headed back home to Atlanta, Georgia.

"Sis, let me know when you make it," she told her best friend and they separated going to their terminals.

Farren called Kool because for some reason she had been missing him since the night they chilled. She knew what it was and she didn't care to admit that she was somewhat attracted to Kool because he reminded her of Christian.

"Wasup shawty," he answered the phone quickly.

"How did you know it was me?" she asked.

"I got ya number saved. What it do?" Kool told her. Farren's soul clenched, she loved the way dudes from Atlanta talked. It was something about that Southern drawl that turned her on.

"Not much, headed out of town real quick," she told him.

"When are you coming my way?" he asked.

"Are you scheduled for a meeting any time soon?"

"Nah, but I want to finish our conversation from the other night. If that's okay with you?" he asked.

"Yeah, I gotta get you to fall in love Mr. I just want the money," she joked.

"I'm good on all that shawty, just let me know when you're headed my way," he said.

"Will do," she told him.

Farren called her mom and told her to keep an eye on Jonte for her as she boarded her plane. Until they officially called it quits, Jonte would not be parading that hoe around Hardy projects as long as her name was tagged to his ass.

Chapter Four

Farren was not looking forward to meeting with Mr. Bianchi at all, she knew who killed Christian Knight, and her heart told her it was Greg. The only thing she needed help figuring out was if Mr. Bianchi ordered Greg to do it and was that why he got his seat at The Cartel so that he could vote Christian out, because Mr. Bianchi knew that he needed one more vote…there were so many unanswered questions and Farren knew she had to put the pieces of the puzzle together real quick, before something detrimental happened.

As soon as her plane landed, Jeff was there to take her to the hotel.

"Do you know what this meeting is about?" she asked.

"Like I told you before, I should have got out when your dad passed, too many new faces." He shook his head.

"Jeff, there's no way for me to leave? Are you sure?" she asked.

"No, there isn't. I'm sorry," he told her.

Farren was grown as hell and she wasn't nobody's bitch. She didn't like what she did and she didn't want to do this forever, she just didn't.

Farren needed sex. It had been so long since she'd been stroked, but as long as Jonte's ass was cheating she wouldn't be giving him any of her sweet pussy. She only came for loyal niggas who deserved it and unfortunately her baby daddy didn't deserve it all.

Farren sat in the back seat, praying for a peaceful meeting. She planned on asking Mr. Bianchi for a silent exit. She didn't want to be a part of The Cartel, she never did. After she fulfilled her father's contract, she should have left then.

After showering and preparing for her meet with Mr. Bianchi, she headed to his estate.

As usual, Farren was patted down and led to a room as she waited on Mr. Bianchi to enter the room.

"Hello Farren. How are you?" he asked.

"Well," she told him. Farren didn't bother to stand up as she normally did whenever he entered a room.

In fact, she didn't even turn around to acknowledge him.

He came behind her and twisted her neck around, "Bitch, don't be disrespectful," he whispered.

Farren bit her tongue, this is not how she predicted this meeting to begin.

"I'm sure your father taught you how to treat me, don't forget it. He's not here to rescue you nor is that sorry ass excuse of a husband. Oh and here's a warning, stop talking to Mario. I don't like him and if I were you I would tell your little friend Jeff to stop looking at plane tickets to other countries. There is no where he can go to escape. The Cartel is global. Do you hear me?" he said, sitting in front of her, and fixing himself a drink.

Farren's heart was beating so fast that it was ridiculous, angry wasn't even the word to describe how she was feeling right now. She wanted to come across the table and slice that cracker's neck, she was so pissed off.

Her whole life, she gave respect because she expected respect in return. For him to put her hands on her was the ultimate sign of disrespect.

"Now, I wanted to meet with you because your calendar has been really light lately and we need you in China for a few weeks overseeing this new mass production company until I can find someone to do it. I remember your father telling me before that you handle your business well."

"I have children in case you forgot, and for no one will I be away from my kids for such a long period of time. The longest I will stay gone is a week," she told him. Farren didn't fear many things in life, so if he thought she was about to become his puppet, he might as well had killed her now because no is no.

"I don't care what you have. Do we need to have another repeat of your eldest daughter?" he asked

And that there was the final strike. Farren knocked over everything over and stood up with tears in her eyes.

"You got me fucked up!" she yelled.

Instantly, his guards came out of nowhere and had her in a chokehold. "Let me go!" she yelled and fought.

Mr. Bianchi used his handkerchief in his suit pocket to wipe the Hennessy off of his face, he lit a cigar and walked up to Farren. She was being restrained by his guards.

"I always thought you were a pretty lil bitch," he told her.

Farren's chest heaved up and down. "Fuck you," she told him.

"I could…better than Dice, better than Christian Knight…better than that lil cunt you have playing house husband," he told her, laughing.

"How pretty would you look if I burned your face with this Cuban cigar?" he asked, waving the cigar very close to her face.

Farren tried to move her face, but the guard had his hands clenching her face in place.

"Farren, why all of a sudden are you trying to defy me?" he asked.

"I don't want to do this," she told him.

Farren refused to beg for her freedom, but damn if she wasn't about to plead.

"Why? There are plenty of women who would love to be a part of The Cartel, this life is so secure," he told her.

"It's not the life for me. I didn't choose this life," she told him.

"Give me fifty million, you can leave then," he told her, smiling.

How in the world did this nigga know every fucking thing? That was an estimated amount of how much money she had accumulated in her accounts. She had a few million in other accounts and some more lil money in accounts in her children's names.

Farren contemplated… Could she get her money back up if she was to pay her way out?

Would she end up struggling?

Farren could easily go back to work, but she had become very comfortable tripping.

The businesses that she and Jonte owned were doing fairly well, but it was little money. Farren didn't spent outrageous amounts of money anyway, but it was the fact that she was about to give the bulk of her funds away just to ensure she wouldn't have to live an illegal life.

Farren believed that whatever goes up eventually comes down. Although The Cartel felt as if they were untouchable, doesn't mean that they are. Somebody someday is going to bring all their trifling asses down and she had to get out before it happened. Farren trusted her gut, she always did because it never failed her.

"You don't have long to decide, I want my money by Friday. Now get the fuck out before I have my dog fuck you," he told her. The guards pushed her constantly until she ended up on the front steps.

Farren dusted her pants off and attempted to regain her dignity, she was really feeling some type of way and she had a lot to think about.

She was basically about to hand over her stability, her cushion for rainy days. Damn was it worth it? She knew it was, but still she had a lot to think about...

Jeff got out the car to help her to the truck. "Get in the car, I'm fine," she yelled at him. He didn't understand what was wrong with her until he saw how distraught she appeared to be now seeing that her eyeliner and mascara was all over her face and her clothes were all over her body. Farren Knight didn't look like the Farren Knight that entered the Bianchi estate an hour ago.

Farren checked under the vehicle for any bombs, she wasn't taking any chances. She really didn't want to get in the car and she told him that she wasn't.

"What you mean? Farren, I've been sitting in this car since you got out," he told her.

"Nah, I'm good I'll walk," she told him, shaking her head.

"Farren, it's too hot to be walking," he said.

She threw up the deuces and started the half a mile journey it took to get back to the main road to even get out the neighborhood.

Farren took her heels off and walked bare feet, finding that she didn't have any service on her phone as she tried constantly to call for a cab.

Jeff drove along side of her asking her to get in the car, he was cracking up laughing. Mr. Bianchi had poor Farren tripping. "Girl get in the car, ain't nothing going to happen to you." He hung out the window while he drove.

Farren called Mario to see if her phone was tripping or the cab company's number just wasn't working.

"Yo," he answered on the second ring.

Farren went to tell him to come get her, but before she could a massive explosive went off.

BOOM!!!!!!!!!!!

The impact knocked her on her ass. Minutes later, she had finally came back to reality from the shock of the explosion. She stood in tears watching the small car go up in flames right along with her father's long time bodyguard and driver, Jeff.

Farren wondered what the fuck was going on and why Mr. Bianchi would want to kill her.

Although she felt bad for Jeff, she was happy as hell that she didn't get out that car, how crazy would it be if her children had to bury their mother a week after saying good bye to their daddy.

Mario had been blowing up Farren's phone up back to back. She heard it ringing, but couldn't find it in the grass alongside the street.

Finally she found it. "Where the fuck are you?"

"I don't know. I'm not far from Bianchi's house," she cried.

"Sit tight, lay low, but sit tight. I'm on the way," he told her.

"Don't hang up, I'm scared. Don't hang up," she told him.

"Calm down, I'm on the way. I promise," he assured her.

Farren had to get the fuck on, she didn't like this life. She wasn't built for all the bullshit and back stabbing. She was as real as they came. If she had a problem with you she was coming at you, she wasn't sending anybody to your front door or none of that.

It seemed like forever before Mario came pulling up, by this time many cars had surrounded the burning car. She said a silent prayer for Jeff before Mario turned the car in reverse and they left.

She said nothing. Farren was so overwhelmed with emotion, her feelings were so hurt and she needed some direction.

Mario rubbed her back and told her everything was going to be okay.

He knew she was too shaken up to talk right now, so he let her cry in silence.

Mario parked in his garage and told Farren to get out, she was so hesitant.

"Nobody knows about this spot, I promise," he told her, holding his hand out.

Farren finally took his hand and she got out the car, and allowed him to escort her through his home.

"You want some water or something? I have wine," he offered.

She shook her head, no. All she wanted was her life back and she wished that Christian Knight was here to tell her what to do. He knew these pussy niggas better than she did, and she needed Christian to separate the real from the fake.

She remembered a conversation they had at Ruth's Chris, when she told him how fond of Mario she was.

"Mario is running things now? Damn, I'm getting old," he said.

"He's sweet, and handles his business well," she said.

Christian stared at Farren, knowing her better than she knew herself.

"Y'all fucking?" he asked.

"Christian, do not play with me. Hell no. I don't mix business with pleasure and you know that," she told him, getting offended.

"Why you get so mad?" he asked, laughing.

"What made you ask me that?" Farren asked.

"If y'all aren't fucking then, why are you getting so defensive?" he asked.

"I'm not," she told him, rolling her eyes.

"Let me find out," he teased.

"Let you find out what Chrissy?"

"That you giving that young man some ass, I taught him everything I knew. His father is an outstanding man," he said.

"I can tell, just on how highly he speaks of his father," she told him.

"Yeah The Cartel is changing, everybody out for blood, and everybody trying to be number one. That's why he didn't want me to leave because he knew I was the last of the realest," Christian said.

Farren replayed that conversation in her head over and over again, trying to find some context clues to understand what was going on. Mario sat across from her, staring at her, waiting on her to talk.

"Earth to Farren." He waved his hands across her face.

"I can't believe he just blew up in front of me, like really blew up in front of me. Wow," she said in disbelief.

"Why were you at Bianchi's house?" he asked.

"For a meeting," she told him quietly.

"He said fifty million to leave."

"Fifty million? Wow, that's a deal. I wish he would offer me that," he said.

"You wanna leave?" she asked shocked to hear him say that.

"Yeah, I do. I don't wanna do this forever. I want to go to bed for once knowing that the FEDS ain't running up in there," Mario told her, he never admitted that to anyone.

In the Sanchez family, The Cartel was the only career path, even for his sisters. They weren't allowed to go off to college and make something of themselves.

The family asked Mario all the time when was he having children to carry the legacy way on after all of them had went to Glory, and Mario would always say soon…once he found a wife.

But the truth was, he would never ever bring kids into this world as long as he was a part of The Cartel.

He remembered being at the funeral for Farren's daughter and hearing Farren's cry long before he really knew who she was and his heart was filled with pain. He promised himself then that he would never have children as long as he did business with The Cartel.

The Cartel loomed you in with promises of security and stability for family generations to come, but the truth was they didn't care about you. In fact, the one time you pissed them off or was short with your re-up money they would bash you and spread lies about you to the other families.

Mario admired Christian because he made them respect him. The other families looked down on Christian Knight just like they looked down on Dice when he was first sworn in, whenever you didn't belong to a family, they didn't fuck with you. You were considered an outsider because who was your loyalty to? Nobody but yourself.

Dice came in, stayed to himself and he got shitted on because Mr. Bianchi's son was extremely jealous of the growing relationship between Dice and Bianchi.

Christian was hated because he was the shit, literally. Christian Knight never socialized with any of the families. He handled his business and he handled it well and everyone hated him for it.

He always spoke up and never bit his tongue, but he did it with class so much class.

Mario remembered being a young buck and observing Christian Knight leave his home with so much suave. He always stopped to shake his hand and he shook his hand real firm too.

Christian Knight would always leave young Mario with nuggets of wisdom and everything that Christian Knight told him, Mario definitely saw it playing out one way or the other.

"Leave then," Farren told him.

"I wish it was that simple. The Sanchez family has been in The Cartel for many years," he told Farren.

"I'm paying that fifty million and getting the hell on," she told him.

"What did he want?" Mario asked.

"He told me that he doesn't like you that's for sure," she told him.

Mario was very surprised to hear that because as far as he could go back and recall, the Sanchez family and the Bianchi's had always been at peace.

"I don't give a fuck who he does not like. That new dude is his lil bitch," Mario spat.

Farren ears perked up then, "Who?" she asked.

"Christian's Knight old partner. The families are very upset that he has been invited in," he told Farren.

Damn now Farren was contemplating on staying in just to make sure they exile Greg's ass, but as long as he was in Mr. Bianchi's good graces there was no way it was happening.

"I need to smoke, I'm stressed," she said running her hands through her hair.

"How did you know not to get in the car?" he questioned.

"Something was off about the whole meeting. He kept making lil hints about my daddy and Dice, then he had the nerve to bring my daughter up…" her voice trailed off and got weak just thinking about the disrespect she had endured.

Farren was honestly still lucky to be alive, she knew without a doubt that if they wanted her dead she would be dead right now.

"That's crazy how you just knew that...are you psychic?" he asked. Mario was cool and all, but he was privileged. She wondered without his security did he have heart to stand tall.

She laughed, "Psychic my ass, I'm from the hood. You always know when some shit is about to go down in the hood when ain't nobody outside. You gotta look for all the signs and stay on your toes. Let me tell you something Mario, I don't care where I'm at, hair salon, nail shop, even if I'm at the circus with my kids. I always sit somewhere my back isn't facing the entrance or the exit. I need to see everything," she schooled him.

Farren ain't play that shit and she was far from a dummy. She had dated nothing but straight hood niggas and killers growing up. Dice taught her the game and Christian showed her how the game could be used to produce legit money.

Dice was hood rich, he didn't have nothing to really show for his hard work. Christian Knight was wealthy, he had tons of land, stock, accounts, businesses and everything. His money was flipped multiple times to produce more income for him and his family.

Farren always told young girls, and even women her age who asked for relationship advice, if a nigga can't give you a thousand dollars, hell if he couldn't even give you a hundred then you need to be finding you a new man. If you can't learn something from the man you're sleeping with, then you need to be finding you a new man. If the man that you consider to be the love of your life ,can't put you in a position to better yourself and to elevate from where you are now, then you need to be finding you a new man.

Often times, women like to settle for less than they deserve in fear of being alone or single. It's better to be alone than to waste time, because time is always money.

"You're crazy," Mario told her.

"Hey, but I'm still alive," she told him, and that was nothing but the truth.

Farren needed to talk to Mr. Bianchi again, she needed to know that after she gave him literally all the money she had that he would leave her the hell alone. She didn't want him coming back to haunt her years later, saying he need a favor and all that.

Farren asked, "Do the other families have a problem with me? Am I wanted or something?" she asked.

Mario laughed, "Hell no, your father was a very loved man amongst the families. That's a sign of disrespect to fuck with you," he told her.

"So why is Bianchi charging me to leave?" she asked

"At least you get to leave though. Do you need money?" he asked.

She wanted to tell his rich ass hell yeah, let me get twenty mill, but her pride was something serious.

"Nah, I'm good," she told him. Farren always made a way out of no way, and this time would be nothing different. She knew how to bounce back from any situation and come out on top, she wasn't known as the underdog in law school for nothing.

Farren told Mario she needed a ride back to the airport.

She wanted to go home, she needed to go home. After talking to Jonte briefly with him telling her that the kids were outside playing and everything was taken care of and there wasn't no motherfuckers running up in there, she decided to go to Atlanta. She had a few more questions that needed to be answered and she knew Kool could answer them. She really needed to talk to the head honcho in charge, which was Mr. Bianchi. However, Farren felt like they both needed time to cool off and she decided that she would be in touch with him soon, just not right now.

Farren didn't tell Kool she was coming. She caught a cab to Ashley's house, knocked on the door and her longtime boyfriend answered.

"Farren, what a pleasant surprise. Was Ashley expecting you?" he asked. Farren still couldn't believe her best friend had found happiness with a white man, but she didn't judge. As long as she was happy, Farren was happy.

"No, I won't be here long though. Are y'all about to go out?" she asked, stepping into the home.

"Yeah for dinner. Ash, you have a surprise," he shouted. Farren made her way to Ashley's room, but the sounds coming from the bathroom made her open the door only to see her friend was standing over the toilet throwing up.

Farren rushed to her side and saw that Ashley's mouth was filled with blood, Farren went to call out to Ashley's boyfriend and Ashley grabbed her hand.

Her eyes pleaded with her to be quiet, Farren went to close and lock the bathroom door, and she opened the linen closet and started running hot water over a washcloth.

She took her time being there for her friend, as she had always been there for her over the years.

Minutes later, "So are you going to tell me what that was about?" she asked.

"I will when we get back. Are you staying?' she asked, sadly.

"I wasn't planning on it, but I damn sure am staying now," she told her matter-of-factly.

"Okay sis, I promise I will update you. He doesn't know yet, and he's really been looking forward to tonight," she said.

"I understand," Farren hugged her tight.

Ashley's boyfriend called her name out for a second time.

"Let me go," Ashley told Farren.

"Do you mind if I borrow your car?" Farren asked.

"Sure sis, keys are in the kitchen," she told her.

"You're looking good, girl," Farren complimented her best friend.

"I'm sick as hell," she whispered before leaving the bathroom.

She wasn't prepared to talk about whatever Ashley needed to tell her, she'd rather wait until she could get all of the story. She just prayed that whatever her friend needed to tell her, it was able to be fixed.

Farren took a bubble bath in the guest bathroom after she made sure the alarm was on and all of the doors were locked. She smoked a blunt as she sat in the tub and her gun was right where she could reach it. Farren also had a chair perched under the door, she wasn't playing no games.

Her bubble baths have always been a very important of her day. No matter how bad Farren's day was, whether she had failed a test or lost a case in court back in the day, a bubble bath would fix everything for her.

This was the first bubble bath she couldn't really enjoy because she had so much on her mind. Farren also felt like somebody was coming for her, she didn't want to be paranoid or having to constantly look over her shoulder, which is why she needed to go see Mr. Bianchi ASAP. Farren lived a peaceful life, and she stayed on the go entirely too much to be scared to leave the house.

Farren got out the tub quickly after realizing the bubbles weren't relaxing her or calming her down.

She called Kool, secretly missing him and wanting to be in his presence.

"Miss Lady, what it do?' he answered.

"Hi, how are you?" Farren asked.

"What's wrong?" his voice super alert.

How did he know something was wrong? See, that's what she liked, someone super in tune with her emotions.

Jonte used to be and he still is to a certain point, his mind was just on other bitches right now and Farren wasn't having it all.

She took a deep breath.

"YO?" he called out, because Farren never responded to his question.

"Come to me," she whispered into the phone.

"Say no more, send me the address. You need something?" he asked.

"Just you," she told him.

Kool promised he was on his way, he literally dropped everything he was doing, took his homeboy back to his car and made his way to Alpharetta.

Although, Farren's location was definitely out of his jurisdiction, being that the police in Alpharetta were known for pulling over black men, he still made his way to shawty.

Farren answered the door in a big t-shirt and her gun.

She didn't give a fuck, until further notice the gun was going everywhere she was going.

"What's with the weapon?" he asked, after he locked the front door and followed her into Ashley's den.

"Whose house is this?" he asked.

"My best friend lives here, she's not here right now though," Farren told him.

"Aye put that gun down…down," he told her, once she noticed Farren still had the gun in her hand even though she was sitting on the couch, wine glass in one hand and .44 in the other.

"Today was long," she told him.

"I'm listening. Can I smoke in here?" he asked.

Farren nodded her head, then went on to tell him everything that happened.

"So what are you going to do?" he asked.

"Pay the money I guess." She shrugged his shoulders.

"Then what?"

"What do you mean?" Farren asked.

"You gone pay them all this money and then what? They're going to be able to come to your house and fuck with you when they want too. Not worth it" he told her, taking a pull on his blunt.

"Kool, he wants me to go to China. Fucking CHINA for months. I have kids. I can't go to China," she told him.

"You can work something out, you've been working it out," he told her.

"I need Jesus." Farren leaned her head back on the couch, she felt so defeated.

"I don't really fuck with them niggas. I pick up the work and that's it," he said.

"Do you regret joining?" she asked him.

Kool shook his head. "Nah shawty, I'm in my own lane and it's going to stay that way," he said.

"I just wish I never would have gotten myself into this situation. Chrissy told me that they were shady. He told me over and over again," she told him.

"How have you been? You looked real nice at the funeral too," he complimented her.

"Thank you, I'm just staying busy. Trying not to think about it, honestly," she said.

"I saw your dude there. How long y'all been kicking it?" he asked.

"Few years, it's not what you think," she told him.

"Oh really? What do I think? Please let me know shawty," he said.

"We're cool, we're co-parenting, and my children love him," she admitted.

"And do you love him?" he asked.

"Yeah I do, but not in that I wanna be with you forever type way." It felt so good to Farren talking to someone else, opening up and being honest.

"What's the difference?" Kool asked.

"It means, that I can love and care for you from a distance, I wouldn't fuck him again," she kept it all the way one hundred.

Kool raised his eyebrow." Why though?" he asked.

"He's disloyal, I have no respect for him," she told him, which was true. Farren refused to be with someone who couldn't be her one and only.

"I feel that, that's why I don't have no bitch, man. I ain't got time."

"Why she gotta be a bitch? Why can't she be your girl or your lady?" Farren asked.

"That's just what I say, I don't mean nothing by it," Kool told her.

"So if I called your mother a bitch would that be okay?"

"Watch your mouth shawty," he warned.

"Okay then, that's what I thought," she said.

"I couldn't date you, fall in love with you. Whatever you call it," he said.

"And why is that? Not that I find you attractive or anything, I'm just asking a question," she questioned.

"Mouth too smart. I'll be fucking you up on the daily," he told her, looking dead in the eyes.

"Hmm, we will see," she said, biting her lip.

Kool looked over at Farren and stared intently at her. Man, she was so fine, he just had to play it cool.

"Why you sitting all the way over there?" he asked. He respected her, so he wouldn't take her to fast.

"I'm chilling right here. Man bring your ass over here and stop playing," Kool commanded.

Farren tried to act like she was unaware of what was about to go down and the angel in her told her to ask him to leave before she was forced to commit a few sins. Her body was yearning to be touched, kissed, licked and spanked too. She wanted to be loved and told that everything was going to be okay.

Farren wanted her body to feel like it was on fire, she wanted to inhale and exhale sex all night. She wanted her back to be arched so low and ass so high up in the air.

Farren wanted her tongue and lips to be sucked on, she desired to be held. Farren wanted to wake up limping, passion marks all over her body.

She wanted someone to stare in her eyes and tell her that she mattered. See, there was a difference between being fucked and made love to. Being fucked was cool and all. Don't get it twisted, every now and then women wanted their hair pulled and to be a choked just a lil bit. But for the most part, after a long stressful week, especially with all of the bullshit that Farren had endured. She wanted her pussy to be eaten, she wanted it to be devoured inside and out. She wanted to feel like she was the only person that mattered in the world, to someone, to somebody. Farren wasn't sure that when she woke up she was the first person on Jonte's mind. Farren could accept that if he woke up thinking about money, but damn could she be the second thought.

Could she be a priority again? Could she be the love of his life? His lady, his wifey?

Farren wanted to feel like somebody wanted her and she wanted to feel appreciated.

The beginning is always when the most memories are made, and now it just seemed like they were only concerned with the well-being of their children. They stopped caring about each other and working on their relationship. Most importantly, Jonte failed to keep the only promise she asked for and that was to stay loyal.

Farren could deal with a lot of shit in a relationship because she had put up with so much in previous relationships, but the one thing that her tolerance had always remained low was disrespect.

Farren didn't do well with disrespect, because she was raised to respect the peasants, the pimps and the prostitutes. When Farren was little her mama would slap her silly if she told Pam the local crackhead in Hardy Projects, "yeah" instead of "yes ma'am". Her mother always told her the same heads you stepped on to get to the top would be the same ones you pass by when you go crumbling back down.

When Jonte started parading Trina around the hood as if he didn't have a fiancée at home was the final straw, especially when she saw it for herself. That was the worst feeling ever.

Farren hadn't given herself time to cry and lay in her misery because time was money and she had a lot of loose ends to wrap up right now, she would do all of that later.

Kool called out her name three more times, but Farren was super caught up in her feelings right now. He came over to her and stood over her and held his hands out, she took his hands in hers and she stood making eye contact with him.

"What?" she asked.

"Whatever you're thinking about, postpone it till tomorrow. You with me now," he told her.

Damn if this nigga didn't remind her of Dice and Christian Knight, wrapped in one perfect man. Farren wondered what his flaws were, what were his setbacks…oh she instantly remembered, he didn't believe in love.

Hell at this point Farren didn't either. So with that thought being pushed to the back of her head, she took her clothes off and Kool was just looking at her.

"What are you doing?" he asked, super surprised at her straight forwardness.

"Skipping all the bullshit, and giving you what you want," she told him, unbuckling her pants.

"How you know that's what I want?" he asked, licking his lips.

Farren turned around and slid her pants down, exposing her blush thong. "Oh don't act," she told him, winking her eye.

"Shit, that's all you?" he asked. There was no way, this lady was in her late 40's with an ass like that. Lawd have mercy. Kool didn't eat ass, but the way she had his dick rock hard, he wanted to put his whole face in it.

Farren laughed, "Oh my God, yes it is," she said, smacking her own ass. But the smack wasn't hard enough for Kool, he liked to leave handprints.

"Come here, you gotta do it like this," he told her as he brought his hand all the way back, and slapped her right ass cheek causing it to jiggle and turn red.

"Ouch!" Farren yipped in pain, it really did hurt.

Kool bent her over the couch, and fished for a condom in his back pocket. He probably didn't have many, but he knew he had at least one.

And he did, he took his time stroking his dick to keep it hard and he put the condom on and used his other hand to rub his fingers between Farren's legs. He thought she may have needed a lil help getting wet, but baby girl was already soaking.

"Damn shawty, you don't even need my help," he whispered.

Farren took a deep breath as he entered her, she was thankful that he took his time with her because she knew that she was extra tight.

"Hmmmmm," she moaned quietly.

Kool took his time working his hips, her pussy was good as fuck.

"Shawty, ain't no way this pussy biting back like this," Kool told her, smacking her ass and gripping it all at the same tight.

Farren's pussy was squeezing the life out of his dick every time he stroked her. His eyes constantly rolled to the back of his head and his toes were curling up something serious.

She was throwing it back, and twerking all over his dick.

Farren got lower on the couch, lifting her ass up high enough for her to slide her arm in between his legs and she fondled his balls as he continued to fuck her real slow and sweet.

"Hell yeah, keep doing that," he told her. Kool stuck his finger in her ass and fingered her.

Farren didn't like the added pressure that it brought to her, but Kool told her, "Trust me shawty, that nut is gonna feel so good. I promise bae."

So Farren closed her eyes and tried to enjoy the new feeling, eventually she loosened up and allowed him to bring her to an awesome climax.

Kool came right after her, silently depositing his release into the condom.

They caught their breaths, slowly but surely.

"Whew," she said, laying on the floor, wiping sweat from her forehead.

Kool sat his naked body on the couch, and lit his blunt back up.

He said nothing. He was a quiet man, which made Farren uncomfortable.

"You good? You need some water?" she asked.

"Nah, I'm good," he told her in a hushed tone.

Farren felt awkward, she reached to get the throw blanket that was laying over the other couch, to cover her body.

"What you doing? Nah, you don't need that," he told her.

"Umm you're just staring at me not saying nothing," she told him.

"Cus you're so beautiful to me, man," he told her.

"Whatever. You got it now, don't start spitting game. You ain't been doing it," Farren brushed him off.

"Damn, that's how you feel?" he asked.

"I'm just keeping it real," she told him.

"Come over here with me," he told her.

Farren scooted towards him, Kool motioned her to stop. "Now lay back," he told her.

Farren was looking super confused. "Lay down," he told her.

She laid down, legs closed and hands down by her side. "Now open your legs," he told her. Kool sat on the edge of the chaise right in front of her, smoking his blunt, in nothing but his wife beater and Nike socks.

"Play with that pussy and stare at me. Don't take your eyes off of me," he told her.

This freak! Farren was so nervous, but after a while she loosened up and really got into it. Before she knew it she was screaming and bucking all over the floor, sweet cum was all in between the middle of her fingers and all down her hands.

Kool got in between her legs and kissed her lips.

"I don't like kissing, but I wanna kiss you," he told her.

"Kiss me then and shut up," she told him.

He smothered her face and took his time kissing her. He even took it up a notch and cleaned her hand with his tongue.

Kool fingered her slowly and made her call out his name. Farren was feeling so damn good, she didn't even hear Ashley and her boyfriend coming in.

"Sis? You need me to leave," she asked, standing in the living room.

"Oh my! Ashley, I'm sorry. I'm so sorry," she told her, hopping up.

Ashley covered her boyfriend's eyes. "Farren, we're going to stay at his house tonight. You and your friend be careful," she laughed.

A few seconds later, she heard the door locking and Kool went back to kissing her. "Hold on, wait. Give me a second," she told him.

Farren couldn't believe she just fucked a nigga she did business with, that was the ultimate no-no, plus she was tired of talking to street niggas.

Farren always attracted the same man then wondered why she was left with a broken heart, she needed to switch some shit up to get different results.

"You good?" he asked her.

"Yeah, I'm about to go to bed," she told him being short.

It didn't take much for Kool to get the hint that his presence was no longer being requested, he got dressed.

Farren walked him to the door. "Just call me shawty when you're ready to talk, no pressure," he told her, kissing her forehead and leaving.

Farren locked the door behind him, threw her t-shirt on over her head and cried herself to sleep. She enjoyed herself with Kool tonight, but no matter who she attempted to like or be with there was always that tiny ounce of guilt and depression lingering in the back of her mind. She felt that she would never be worthy of love because she had fooled around with Dice knowing he was a married man. She didn't even feel like being with anybody else right now. For what? Love never lasted long for her.

Farren lacked in an area that she knew nothing about, apparently she was doing something wrong. She wouldn't even give Kool the chance to break her heart, she wasn't in the mood to get played, and Farren was getting too old to be dealing with bullshit and crying over a man.

Chapter Five

Farren and her mother were having lunch, she was attempting to put the pieces of her messed up life back together. Jonte was coming home every night that never changed. Farren knew that he was only there because he loved those kids, he barely said two words to her. It was like he knew that she had fucked off on him. Farren knew she had no physical signs of her fucking Kool, but she would be lying if she said he didn't leave a mental mark on her. She kept thinking about him, and every time she called him, she hung up. Kool ended up texting her one night, tired of Farren playing on his phone and he told her, "Stop playing games with me. We are both grown. The next time you call me and hang up, I'm going to block you."

Farren never responded to his message because she didn't know what to say, she knew she needed to stop. She was wondering if he was talking to someone else, or did he even miss her.

Farren had accepted Christian's death the best way she knew how to, she told herself that everything happened for a reason. Her time with Christian had come to an end a very long time ago, way before he had passed. Farren knew she needed to let it go. She had gotten over Dice's death and she knew that one day she would really be 100% okay.

Her mother spoke up, "So you paid that dummy fifty million dollars to sit around and do nothing all day?" her mom asked.

"Not sit around, spend time with my children, start back gardening, and I've took on a few cases. I'm having fun," she told her mom.

Nakia wasn't a dummy at all, she knew that Farren had begun to enjoy her new life, traveling all over the world. Farren's mother knew how that thrill and power that only The Cartel could give you felt like, she knew it all too well...

"Girl please, ain't nothing going on Jersey," she told her daughter.

"Ma, I can't believe you're mad that I left."

"I'm not mad at all, I just think your reasons are stupid. I know good and damn well Bianchi is going to be calling you," she said.

Mario had told Farren the same thing, Farren hoped that he didn't because that life was behind her.

The only thing that Farren didn't put behind her was killing Greg, somehow someway he had to die.

He didn't deserve to live at all.

"Well hey, the sacrifices I had to make as a mother and I would do it again with the quickness," she told her mom and rolled her eyes.

"When was the last time you to spoke to that girl?" her mom asked.

"Ma, what girl?" she questioned. Her mom was always randomly asking questions, she was starting to get old.

"Amari, Jonte's sister in law?"

"I don't really fool with her like that," she said.

"Watch her, it's something about her. I can't put my finger on it, but it's something about her that I do not like and I told Jonte this the other day. He laughed and said I don't like nobody," she told her daughter and shaking her head at the same time.

There were a lot of people back in the day that trusted Farren's mom judgment. All the big dope dealers would stash their drugs at her house and count money for them.

Farren's mom also used to sell her assumptions for what she thought the numbers were going to be for that day. She made a few thousand off of her assumptions way back when.

Her mother's opinion had always been trusted. Many people thought that it was Farad, Farren's father, who was super wise. However, it was he who confided in Nakia for everything.

Nakia had made lasting relationships with a lot of people in The Cartel, all except Bianchi. He didn't like Nakia and damn sure didn't like her daughter or anyone associated with them.

Farren asked her mom, "What made you say you don't like her?" It wasn't that she wasn't listening to her mom, she just wanted to know what her reasoning.

"Too sneaky for me, I wouldn't be surprised if she was sniffing powder. When have you ever known that girl to hang around Hardy even when her husband was living? I never ever seen her in Hardy, now every other day she is leaving somebody's house," she told Farren.

Farren took it all in and she planned on asking Jonte was Mari okay. She was going to invite her to lunch to feel her out. If Mari was on some bullshit, Farren planned on keeping her enemies super close.

Farren's mom asked her, "Chile, are you almost done eating? I'm not trying to be with you all day? I got a date," she said.

Farren laughed. "Honey a date with who?" she asked.

"Don't worry about it, just hurry up."

Farren ate her last two pieces of steak and sipped her water with lemon, she left money for their food and a tip and then she and her mom dipped out of the restaurant.

Chapter Six

"Morgan, blow out the candles baby," Jonte told his daughter, the family were at the home celebrating Morgan's birthday. All she requested was a *Frozen* themed cake and a few of her friends to come over and watch *Frozen* for the millionth time.

Farren was happy that her daughter was happy, Noel thought she was the mama at all times.

"Sit down, we will bring the cake to you," she fussed to one of Morgan's friends.

"No, you sit down," Farren's mom chastised her.

Noel pouted, but she knew not to roll her eyes, she felt Farren staring at her waiting on her to act up.

Farren went and got some more napkins and spoons out of the kitchen. Mari sat at the breakfast bar whispering on the phone. Farren didn't bother to even ask who she was on the phone with because she was a grown woman. Mari chose to not be family-oriented, all day she sat in the kitchen away from everyone. Farren didn't bother to include her, the bitch was super bipolar. Just the other week she was blowing Farren phone up to go get drinks but today she barely said two words to her.

Kim kept telling Farren that she had seen her out before with some, dude but she didn't know his name. Farren told Kim that she didn't care, today was all about her daughter and nothing else mattered.

"Daddy, when are we opening my gifts?" Morgan asked.

"Whenever you want to princess," he told her.

Farren snapped a few candid photos of today's event, there were so many perfect memories to be captured.

"Are you okay?" Farren's sister, Neeki asked her.

"Yeah, why you ask?"

"You look sad," she told her.

"Just thinking about Ashley, I wish she was here," Farren had discovered before she traveled back to her home in Jersey that Ashley had been diagnosed with stage three stomach cancer and it was pretty aggressive. All she could do was promise to be there for her best friend, Farren didn't know what she was going to do without her number one supporter if God forbid something had happened to her.

Ashley was that friend that didn't call every day, not even every week, but you knew without a doubt, that she was your very best friend. Ashley never missed an important accomplishment or even the simplest ones. She was always positive and uplifting and never judgmental. Ashley had been Farren's friend way before they both received their degrees or was able to get houses and cars in their own names.

Ashley had held her hand and rubbed her back through Dice and Christian's untimely death, and didn't miss the birth of any of her four children. In fact, she was right with her when she found out she was pregnant with Carren and Morgan.

Ashley was a true friend and at this time Farren had been flying to Atlanta every free opportunity she got to spend time with her and go to the doctor with her.

"Everything will be okay, I promise," Neeki reassured her and gave her a side church hug.

Farren took a deep breath and started bringing all of Morgan's gifts to the living room, so everyone could see her open them.

An hour or two later, the party was coming to an end and Farren couldn't act like she was delighted. She was extremely tired and really needed a nap. She had recently started back taking cases and Farren quickly remembered why she stopped practicing law in the first place; the amount of time that it required. Law was frustrating and extremely time-consuming, Farren barely had enough time for a massage. As soon as she would be getting comfortable, an email would be coming through. She knew deep down in her heart, that this was not something she planned on doing for long.

It wasn't her passion to begin with, but it was a good paycheck so she chose to not complain. There were some people that didn't have a degree to fall back on and luckily Farren had three.

Farren saw the last of her guests out, Jonte and Mari was in the den whispering as usual. Farren normally paid them no mind. She felt that as long they weren't grown enough to speak up about whatever or whomever they were discussing she didn't respect it, but what they weren't going to do was whisper in her home. They could take the whispering down the street or even across town to Hardy Projects for all she cared.

"Excuse me. Mari, thanks for coming to Morgan's party. We are about to shut the house down now and I think your kids are ready to go too," she told her very politely.

Jonte looked over at her, in disbelief that Farren was being so rude.

She ignored his glances, she was tired and didn't want anyone in her house while she took a bath or a nap. Farren didn't trust Mari, the bitch wouldn't catch her slipping.

Mari laughed it off, "Okay boo, go get the kids for me," she told her and turned back around to face Jonte.

"Nah, you can go get your own children. Jonte, see your sister in law out, please. Goodnight," she told Mari and her sorry ass baby daddy.

Farren ran herself a hot steamy bubble bath filled with bath salts and lavender body wash. She planned on sitting in the tub until the polish on her toes peeled.

Farren sipped on red wine as she watched the water fall from the faucet, Jonte entered, "Can we talk?' he asked.

"No," she told him.

He hadn't been wanting to talk, in fact, she couldn't recall the last time they were in a room alone without the kids. Jonte would fall asleep in the guest room and bathe in the guest bathroom. The room was slowly piling up with all of his things. Farren slept alone so much that the side of his bed remained untouched. When she would wake up in the morning to head in to the office, she wouldn't do anything but fold her side back up and reposition the pillows.

When she cooked, she always left him a plate in the microwave since the majority of the time he kept late nights.

The only thing that Farren could respect about Jonte was that he always came home, even if it was four or five in the morning and he was high as all get out. Jonte always made his way home.

"Okay, well you listen and I talk then," he fussed.

She rolled her eyes and undressed, knowing that her killer body was the ultimate distraction for him. Especially since it had been so long since he had touched, smelled her skin or visited in between her legs.

Farren played with herself at night with thoughts of Kool's long and fat dick, Dice's pretty face with his dimples and freckles and Christian Knight's charm, no one had charm like Christian Knight. He was the bomb.com

"I told Trina that I had to stop fucking with her. I'm not trying to lose my family over anybody," he said.

Farren unsnapped her bra and threw it in the dirty clothes hamper, she moved around the bathroom, removing her jewelry. Jonte noticed that she wasn't wearing her engagement ring, it was sad that he was just now noticing because Farren hadn't wore it in weeks.

It had been two months since Christian Knight had passed.

Farren slid in the water, completely ignoring Jonte. She wasn't stunting shit he was talking about, at all.

"Farren?" he called her name.

"Jonte please get out and cut the light off when you leave. Thank you," she told him.

"Farren!" he called out her name again. Why didn't Farren see the seriousness in his eyes, hear the pleading in his voice? She never bothered to look at him, never even really heard him out because she didn't care.

If it took him months to realize what he had at home, then too bad too sad. She had moved on and that was that.

Now they were doing an amazing job at co-parenting and could continue this way, but other than that them as a unit, a couple, becoming one under God…nah, Farren was good on all that love shit.

Her only focus was stacking her money up and being the best mother she could be to her children, she owed them that much.

The constant traveling wasn't unacceptable. As a mother it was Farren's job to keep her children number one in her life and for The Cartel she felt like her kids had taken a back seat. Farren promised to never let that happen again.

"I'm trying to make it work with you. I love you," he told her.

Farren started humming a song, she wanted Jonte to get the hint and leave her the fuck alone.

"I'm not giving up on us baby." He came near the tub, and took the washcloth that was folded by the tub and drawled it down in the water and lathered the washcloth with soap, and began to wash her legs and feet. Jonte didn't care that his clothes was getting wet.

Farren ignored him, Jonte motioned for her to turn around so he can wash her back.

"Jonte, we have come to an end…" she tried to tell him.

"Shhh…baby shhh… Be quiet," he told her.

He took his time washing her body and making sure she was smelling good. Farren was irritated and her face showed it.

Jonte let the water out of the tub, grabbed the pink terry towel that Farren had sat out for her to dry and he held it out for her to step in.

"I got it," she told him, snatching the towel from him.

She wasn't in the mood to be babied. Where was he when Chrissy died? Where was he when she really needed him the most? In Hardy with some young bitch that couldn't even compare to Farren. She was fed up and had no words for him.

Jonte usually would leave her alone when she was being stubborn, but tonight all he wanted was his lady.

He ignored her fussing and dried her off, he then got the lotion out to moisturize her body and he took his time not missing one crevice on her body.

Farren couldn't lie and say that she didn't enjoy the deep massage he was giving her. Jonte took his time kneading out the tights in her body it had been so long since she visited the spa.

Farren moaned once he started rubbing on her ass knowing good and damn well he didn't deserve to even be this close to her.

Jonte bent down and bit both of her ass cheeks, then kissed the very same places that he brought pain to. Farren was enjoying the attention, it had been so long since they spent time together.

She didn't want him to know just how good his hands were making her feel, so she said nothing. She just occasionally let out tiny whimpers.

Jonte led her to the bed and she followed his moves and laid down too.

"I'm not fucking you," she told him.

"Shut up, please just shut up," he told her. He then took his time rubbing his hands through her hair and down her face. He pinched and rubbed on her nipples and replaced his fingers with his tongue and lips.

Farren missed his touch that she refused to deny.

His touch made her weak, made her insecure, made her question if he was gentle with that other girl whose name she refused to ever mutter in her house again.

Trina didn't get that much credit in Farren's book. Any hoe that openly disrespected another woman was like shit in her eyes, literally.

Jonte somehow found the entry to Farren's unforbidden place. In only a few licks he reminded her just how much he loved her by bringing her to a climax so sweet, she couldn't do nothing but beg him to stop.

Jonte knew the kids were still up, so he quickly turned the television on in an attempt to drown out the noise of their mother.

Farren screamed she was cumming from the top of her lungs. With tears in her eyes and the skin that covered her bottom lip damn near peeled off, she cried from the intense feelings that he had dragged out of her.

Farren attempted to catch her breath. Once Jonte finally decided that he had enough of her sweet goodness, she laid back down and tried to breathe.

See, Farren was getting older and couldn't last as much as she used to, so when Jonte entered her with no condom she immediately was brought back to reality. Her hands motioned flag on the play.

Jonte was confused and his dick was rock hard. "Flag on the play buddy. No glove, no love," she told him straight up.

Jonte couldn't remember the last time he and Farren had used protection, but he didn't protest. Although he was pretty sure his body wasn't filled with diseased or any infection, he still reached in the nightstand drawer and covered his dick in latex per his baby mama's request.

Jonte finally was able to enter her and instantly he remembered how he was able to fall in love with Farren so fast. Yeah she was fly as hell, and she had her own, she could cook any meal a nigga asked for, she was clean, educated and prayerful.

But Farren had a monster in between her legs, it captured your mind and pulled you in.

Farren's pussy was a classic piece of art, literally.

It was so beautiful and tight, the noises that it made should have been put on CD for niggas all across the world to bust to. She was so delicate and natural, she didn't try too hard or was she too rough.

The look she gave a nigga back when he was stroking it just right, would instantly cause him to loose count of his strokes, because every nigga know that they counting to ten before they just straight go ham in that pussy.

Jonte felt himself feeling like the *Man of the Year* once Farren's juices coated his dick. Damn, that had to have been her third time cumming in a matter of a few seconds.

He increased his strokes and started dropping those balls off in her, feeling too damn good.

Jonte reached down to kiss her lips only for Farren to move her face out of his way. It was fucked up, but she only wanted to kiss Kool. She knew that he wasn't kissing no other bitches because that wasn't his thing.

Now Jonte on the other her hand, Farren was very unsure.

Jonte took that swerve like a champ, he reached down and kissed all over her neck, trying to leave his mark. Farren knew what his ass was doing and she wouldn't burst his bubble, she just didn't plan on leaving the house until it cleared up.

She could easily work from home, plus she and Kool weren't talking right now anyway. However, she did miss him like crazy.

Farren moaned louder once Jonte started pumping his dick faster into her. He wanted her to get on top, but she acted like she couldn't understand what he was saying. There was no way she was putting in work for his ungrateful, lying, cheating ass.

Of course, Farren was going to get a few nuts out of this sexcapade and she would even allow him to get one or two, but to sweat and be sore the next morning for a man who had barely said two words to her in the last few months… Nah, she had nothing for him. Jonte was not worth her energy.

Finally, he slowed his pace and gave a few more weak strokes before he came into the condom, then pulled out of her and straggled to the bathroom. Farren used her towel that was found on the floor to wipe between her legs. She patted her face with the other end and went to her dresser to slip on a nightie. She didn't bother with her hair because she had an appointment in a few days anyway, so there was no need.

Jonte came back to bed and snuggled against her. She moved over a little, but not enough for him to assume that Farren didn't want him near.

They watched a movie in silence for the remainder of the night and for the first time in a very long time, Jonte had shared a bed with Farren as they lay.

The next morning, Jonte woke Farren up to breakfast in bed and she was very surprised by his overwhelming amount of attention and affection.

She even gave him a kiss once he returned with her coffee. Although she couldn't really enjoy her breakfast in peace because the kids had come in the room and ate more off of mommy's plate than their own, Farren still appreciated his nice gestures.

She thought for a second, he is the father of her child, she already has the ring and he has her name tatted along with thoughts of them staying together.

Jonte knows her very well, it's not like they are strangers to each other.

Farren told herself that she needed to forgive Jonte if he promised to never cheat again and make it work with her baby daddy.

She brainwashed herself to think that she was too old to be starting all over again with Kool. Farren told herself to put Kool in the back of her head and press forward and stay focused on her family.

Although she and Kool enjoyed their one night together, Farren told herself to leave it at that one night in Atlanta, Georgia and to not leave the one she loved for the one that she wasn't even sure enough that she liked.

Farren told herself that she had already had a man at home and she needed to learn how to stop running from her problems and fix them. If Christian Knight's death didn't teach her anything else, it definitely taught her that life was short and death sometimes came with no warning.

Farren needed to cherish the ones that cherished her, it wasn't like Kool had been blowing her up or anything.

After the children ate all of her food, they dipped.

"So y'all don't wanna watch the news with mommy?" Farren asked.

Michael answered," I'm going to play the game."

Noel responded and Morgan just followed, "We are going to play with our dolls, you can come with us," she said. Morgan smiled at her mom, but ran after her sister.

Jonte asked, "Was it good?"

"Yes, thank you," she told him.

Jonte sat the tray on the floor and laid down next to his fiancée. "What are you doing today?" he asked.

"What I'm doing right now, catching up on all my shows, I'm so behind on Scandal and Good Wife" she shook her head.

Jonte nodded, he wanted something. Farren didn't know what, but it was obvious he was beating around the bush.

She looked at him and waited for him to ask his next pointless question but it never came.

So she pressed play on her DVR remote, about ten minutes later he cleared his throat.

Farren took exhaled loudly, and pressed pause. All she wanted to do was to lay in bed and enjoy her day.

"Wasup?" she said.

"I need you to do a solid for me, bae," he said, rubbing his hands together.

"A solid? Jonte what the hell are you talking about?" she asked.

He got closer to her in the bed. "I need you to talk to your peoples about putting me on, Farren. I can't do this sitting around the house shit no more, it's not me," he blurted out.

Wow, Farren was at a loss for words, she couldn't believe this is what he wanted. This dumb ass nigga wanted to go back to the streets. Jonte barely could avoid the police as it was, it was like they kept a squad car on him. It had gotten so bad in the past few months that Jonte couldn't smoke in his car or carry a gun with him because he was always getting pulled over for the simplest of things. That was the real reason why he was always at home early, in his case, home was the safest place to be.

"Are you fucking serious?" she asked him.

But the look on his face told her, he was as serious as a heart attack.

"What about Morgan? What about your children, and Mari's kids, you really gone risk your freedom for a few extra dollars?" she questioned.

"You and I both know with them I'ma be making more than a few extra dollars. You said it yourself, we took a loss with that money you gave them. It's been bothering me," he said.

Farren curled her lip, she wasn't going to allow him to pull her in on his bullshit. "Tae...baby, what am I sitting here doing?" she asked a question.

Jonte was confused as to what his answer was supposed to be. "Chilling," he said.

"Exactly. Do you think I'm really worried about that money? We're good. We are not hurting for anything, trust me," she told him.

Although, Jonte was her life partner, she learned a very long time ago you never let your right hand know what your left hand is doing. Christian Knight and her father left her with tons of money. Farren had no worries at all and if Jonte would stay down with her, he would have no worries either.

"What about Mari, is she good too?" he asked.

"Uh no, she's not. Mari is grown. She needs to go get a damn job. Did she tell you to ask me that?" Farren questioned.

"No she didn't, I'm grown as hell. But that's my family whether you fuck with her or not," he said. Farren heard the irritation in his voice. He was getting frustrated, but she didn't give a damn for various reasons. The answer is no and wouldn't be changing.

Jonte was entirely too hot, the Cartel would never invite him in because he caused too much attention. They was barely fucking with her, and even If they were she wasn't fucking with them Jonte had enough money from his businesses. It was Mari, who she knew was all in his head. Farren would never put her name on the line for Jonte, he sometimes made stupid decisions like the one he was attempting to make now.

"Like I said, we're good," she told him and pressed play on her show, to signify that the conversation was over.

He got off the bed and went into their bathroom to take a shower. About an hour later, he came in the bedroom dressed in all black.

"I'll be back in a few days. I gotta go handle something," he told her and kept walking.

Farren hopped out of the bed so fast and followed him down the hallway yelling obscenities, "Where in the fuck do you think you're going?" she yelled.

Mike pressed mute on the television, it was very rare that he heard his mother curse.

"Get back," he told her.

"I didn't fall in love with you because you were a dumb ass nigga. Are you stupid?" she asked, being sarcastic.

Jonte went through the kitchen drawers looking for something. Farren continued, "You're about to risk your life for your coke snorting sister in law? Really? She don't give a fuck about you, me or our kids. She's spoiled and selfish," she told him.

"What did she do to you? Can you tell me that?" he stopped what he was doing and asked.

"Are you fucking her or something? I'm confused as to when you became her number one cheerleader," she asked, with her hands on her hips.

Jonte wanted slam Farren's dumb ass in the wall, but he would never put his hands on her, plus she was crazy. He didn't have time to have his face all scratched up.

"You think I'm one of them niggas for real? My brother's wife?" he asked her.

"I'm just asking a question, these days you gotta ask," Farren kept it 100.

"I'm not like you, I don't turn my back on family when I get a lil money, that's not how shit goes around my way," he hit a low blow. However, Farren had put those days ways behind with her sister and mother. She didn't even feel the need to argue with him.

"Do you what you gotta do, don't call me when you get locked up. Go kiss your daughters," she told him and walked off.

Farren's day of chasing and begging a nigga to be somewhere they obviously don't want to be were over. If Jonte felt like going to rob someone for a few thousand dollars was going to put Mari in a better situation to take care of her children, then hey so be it.

Instead of him offering to give her one of his businesses, or invest a few thousand dollars into an investment property or some stock, he was about to go risk his freedom like a dumb ass.

For the sake of the kids, she just prayed that he made it home safe and in one piece. Farren enjoyed her day at home, drinking wine and watching all of her favorite shows. Kool crossed her mind, but her pride didn't let her call. She stared at his contact in her iPhone for a few minutes but never pressed call.

Chapter Seven

"Why isn't daddy here with us?" Morgan asked for the millionth time. The children and Farren had spent the last two weeks in Atlanta, Georgia. Ashley's fiancé called Farren one morning and said that Ashley's doctor advised that any of her family come down to say their goodbyes.

Farren's mother and sister also came down last weekend to be with Farren and Ashley. Farren was looking so tired on Facetime, Neeki knew how her sister could get when she was stressing. Farren had finally found peace with the situation and at this point, she just wanted her friend to be free from the pain. Ashley had told Farren one night that it hurt to laugh and smile.

She didn't want to be on any more medicine because she was always sleepy or sedated. The few days she did have left she wanted to spend them with her fiancé, best friend, god-children and she joked saying she had to watch as much *Young and the Restless* as she could before she went to heaven. Farren didn't find that joke funny, but Ashley did.

Farren rolled her eyes, Morgan was really starting to get on her nerves with the same questions every single day. Couldn't she see that mommy was tired and stressed? Farren was running herself thin, seeing about Ashley all day, every day and trying to juggle a few cases via email and fax, along with making sure the kids weren't bored out of their minds in Atlanta.

"Morgan, daddy had to work. Okay baby? Now put your seatbelt back on, we will be back home in a minute," Farren told her from the front seat.

They went to the Zoo and to get some pizza, the kids looked tired of sitting in the house. Ashley told her that it was okay to leave her at home for a few hours, she promised she would be okay.

"I just want my daddy," Morgan kicked her feet and screamed.

Farren counted to ten, she didn't want to spank her child for no reason, and she knew Morgan was probably just irritated and sleepy as they had been in the sun all day.

Her seat bumped up. "Okay lil girl, hit the back of this seat one more time, and I'm pulling the car over and tearing you up!" she yelled.

Morgan screamed louder and cried, "I WANT MY DADDY!"

Michael tuned her out by putting on his beats by Dre headphones, Morgan was entirely too spoiled in his opinion.

Farren fumbled with her iPhone to call Jonte, she had to call him about ten times a day just to get Morgan to stop from crying.

Jonte's phone went straight to voicemail. She assumed he was probably on the other line, so she called back a few more times and every single time it went straight to voicemail.

That wasn't like Jonte to allow his phone to go dead, she scrolled through her contacts and tried to manage to stay straight and narrow on the road at the same time. She searched her contacts to try and find Jonte's other number, she never really had to call it because he always answered when she called.

He didn't answer that phone either.

Farren decided to wait until she got home to call her mom to see if maybe Jonte was in the hood shooting dice and had left his cell phone at her house or in his car.

Morgan never stopped crying. "Ma, can you turn the music up? She's getting on my nerves," Noel whined.

"She getting on mines too, Morgan shut up," Farren fussed and turned the radio up at the same time.

They made their way home, and about time the car was parked, Morgan was knocked out. Michael carried his sister in the house, Ashley was barely making it to the kitchen. Farren dropped her purse to rush to her friend. "What are you doing out of bed?" she helped her to a seat.

"I got tired of sitting in there, I want a glass of wine," she said out of breath.

"Wine? Girl, you can't have any wine," she fussed.

"I miss my wine," Ashley said sadly.

"Let me look on Google, nah my sister is a nurse. Let me call Neeki," Farren said.

She called her sister and Neeki laughed, she had never heard of someone wanting wine. She advised to just add a lil water to it while Ashley wasn't looking, but she didn't think it would do anything harm.

Farren handed her a glass of wine and joined her at the bar in her kitchen, "Aah…" Ashley made small noises of satisfaction. That wine did something to her.

Farren was more of a Patron drinker, but it made her entirely too horny so she rather drink wine to keep her cool, calm and collected.

"How are you feeling today, really feeling?" Farren asked.

"Tired as hell, ready to die," she admitted.

Farren wasn't expecting that response, but she asked for the truth and that's what Ashley gave her.

"Are you scared?" she asked.

Ashley sipped her wine. "Girl no, I've done everything I wanted to do, went to college, pledged, got a plethora of degrees, traveled the world, paid my house and car off, oh and I've had some of the best sex in my life," she giggled.

Farren laughed with her. "So kids and marriage won't make you feel complete before…"Farren didn't know how to say die or death.

"What before I die? You think I should rush down to the courthouse and get married before I die, so I can say, ooh I was married? Girl no, not happening. I like what we've had for the last ten years. He's been my everything and he knows that," she told her best friend.

"So you are telling me in your last days, you still don't wanna be married with kids?" Farren just couldn't believe, well accept that Ashley never wanted kids.

You work hard in life so that your children can experience life better than you did, you stay faithful to God so He can bless you with a good man. Not only did God send Ashley a good man, but he sent her a wealthy one.

"Farren no, some people don't wanna have a whole bunch of kids. I didn't need vows to establish how much I loved my man. It just was never a priority in my life. I chased my career," Ashley told her.

Farren found herself getting a little offended, but she knew that she couldn't. Everyone was entitled to their own opinion. "So what are you trying to say?" she asked.

"That you followed your dreams and I followed mine, nothing more nothing less. Now, may I have another glass?" she asked.

Ashley didn't want to spend her afternoon, discussing kids that she couldn't have right now anyway or getting married, she didn't believe in marriage. What Ashley wanted to say was, "You were married and still got cheated on, so what makes marriage so special," but she knew how sensitive Farren was so she decided not to say anything.

Farren handed her a full glass of wine. "I'm thinking about moving to Atlanta," she told her best friend.

"Wow, really. You would wait until I'm dying to move closer?"

"Can you stop saying that?' she yelled.

Ashley was surprised. "I'm sorry, I'm just trying to prepare myself and prepare y'all too. It's not a surprise and y'all know that it's coming. Don't cry over me, don't have me a funeral, cremate me and go out of town to celebrate my life." She took Farren's hand in hers, and looked at her with tears in her eyes.

"Please don't be sad over me, move on with your life. I'll always be your friend and you know that," she told her.

Farren wiped her tears. "Everybody who I love keeps dying on me. Like damn, I feel like I don't have anybody anymore," she whimpered.

Ashley held her friend close. "Oh boo, don't say that. Farren, we have had some good times together, think about the good times when you feel yourself getting sad. We have had so much fun growing up," she told her best friend, rubbing her back.

Ashley enjoyed life to the fullest and that was the only reason why she wasn't angry or questioning God.

She really believed that God was trying to show Farren something, she wasn't sure what he lesson was but God was attempting to get Farren by herself to tell her something. He was about to separate her from all of the people she depended on for peace, Ashley felt that in her spirit.

Ever since they were little, Farren always wanted someone to walk with her, to ride with her to the store, to go to the mall with her, she could never just go by herself. Not to say that Farren wasn't independent or struggled with being alone. She just always remembered Farren having someone by her side.

Up until Dice's death, she really didn't spend time alone, by herself. She and Ashley were in all the same classes, played all the same sports, the only thing that they didn't have in common were their choice of men. Ashley liked white men, always have and always will.

She didn't like dark skinned men or meat, she loved her dick pink and long. Ashley preferred well-rounded men, men who traveled and spoke well. There weren't too many men who fit her criteria in Hardy Projects. Ashley remained a virgin up until she moved to Atlanta, Georgia for graduate school.

She had been with the same man ever since, he had truly captured her heart.

However, Farren wasn't really content. She was constantly seeking validation for the decisions she made in life.

It wasn't until after Dice died, was she forced to be alone. Ashley was in Atlanta, Georgia and she had completely separated herself from her family after she graduated from high school.

She dealt with Dice's death by herself because she really had no other choice. Dice's family was well aware of who Farren was, but of course, they tended to Dice's wife and children as if she had never came over his mother's house to have dinner too.

Farren casted a web for her to live in, she didn't go out or socialize. She drowned herself in work, school and shopping. She told herself that she was unworthy of love and she just knew she was going to die alone.

Then…Christian Knight came along, super unexpected and out of nowhere.

Farren lost herself in Christian Knight, she lost her sanity trying to keep and please him. Love captured her mind, body and spirit. And for a second time around, she forgot who she was, what she loved to do, and what made her smile because Christian Knight had become her everything.

Once Christian Knight broke her heart, there she goes again…going ghost. Changing her number, hiding out, not talking to anyone, cutting her hair and going ham in the gym. Farren only desired change after someone separated from her, but she wasn't alone in this.

Many women only had epiphanies after the break up, they only realized that they deserve better *after* the nigga leaves them or cheats on them.

Why settle all alone? Why settle for three maybe five years, then realize oh the nigga wasn't shit? When in reality, you knew it all along. You knew all along that he wasn't happy and neither were you. You knew all along that he was fucking around and you were just something to do when there wasn't nothing to do. You knew all along, that he was anxious to hit you with the exit.

Why wait? Why wait till they break your heart or call it quits?

Farren still to this day, continues to say there were no warning signs. She said that she didn't know Christian Knight was unhappy. When in reality, she knew all along, but she didn't want to believe it. She refused to admit that she lost herself in him and couldn't find the strength to walk away, and so she became blind and deaf. She couldn't see his lies and betrayal, she couldn't hear him sneaking around the house on the phone talking to Asia. She refused to observe and witness the bullshit.

So why was she so hurt when he finally left? Because she had been a damn fool.

Farren was then on round two of "changing for the better" once Jonte came alone.

She wasn't expecting him to come into her life, just as she wasn't expecting Dice or Christian.

But Jonte came, Jonte made her smile, Jonte made her laugh, he bought her nice things, he made her promises, and told her he would be with her forever.

Now what? Now Jonte barely answered the phone, and Jonte was riding around the city in a car that Farren bought for him with another bitch.

So where was Farren now?

On round 3 of "changing for the better."

Farren seriously needed to get it TOGETHER, Ashley wanted so bad to tell her that the love she had been so desperately seeking in every failed relationship was hidden within.

Ashley wiped Farren's tears and said, "Sis, you have yourself and your kids, that's really all you need," she told her and gave her a hug.

Farren knew Ashely was only telling her the truth but she had enough shit going on right now to be worried about fixing herself.

They spent the rest of the night catching up and reminiscing on life and the good days.

Farren ended up falling asleep with Ashely in her bed. That wine had her super knocked out, which was a good thing because she hadn't really been getting much sleep.

Of course, as a mother a full eight hours of sleep was unheard of. Morgan came in the room crying for her daddy.

Farren fumbled through her purse, with one eye close to call Jonte. She didn't care that it was six in the morning, if Morgan was going to keep her waking up wanting her sorry ass daddy, then Jonte would be waking up to calm her down.

Both of his phones were still going to voicemail. Farren knew her mom was probably up getting ready for work, so she called the house phone.

"Gal, I've been calling you all night!" she yelled.

"Ma, my phones were on silent. Have you seen Jonte round there? Morgan is about to drive me crazy calling for him," she told her, yawning.

"That fool done got himself locked up yesterday. I guess they had some dope in that girl Trina's house. They ran up in there and got all of em, Spider, Tae, Trina, and Mari," she said.

Farren's heartbeat stopped, literally it came to a complete stop. She couldn't even breathe, her eyes immediately filled up with tears.

"Farren?" her mother called out her name a few times.

"I'm…here…I'm here," she said, coughing and choking. Ashley stirred in her sleep, Farren threw the comforter back and took Morgan's hand and went into the kitchen.

"What is everybody saying?" she asked.

"Well of course it's a wrap for Jonte's dumb ass. He was on his third strike, but I don't know about them other fools," her mom told her.

Farren couldn't believe this shit. "I'll be up there in a few, let me pack our stuff up," she said.

"You need to leave them chirren down there, don't tell them nothing until you get to the bottom of it yourself," she said.

"Ashley can't see about them, especially Morgan," she said.

"Christian's niece is down there, take em over there," her mother told her.

"You're right, let me call Kennedy. Ma, can you book me a flight?" she asked.

"Farren, I don't have no damn computer. Talking about book you a flight," she fussed.

Farren hung up on her mom and called Kennedy who was super excited to spend time with her younger cousins.

"So what exactly happened?" Ashley asked.

"Girl, I have no idea, he's so stupid," she shook her head.

Farren had no choice but to call Kool, Ashley was in no shape to drive and this was the first time she didn't get a rental car. She had been driving Ashley's car around since they had been in Georgia.

"Stranger, what it do?" Kool answered the phone.

"You busy?" she asked.

"Nah, what you want? Cus I know you didn't just up and call me," he said, getting to the point just like she did. Farren didn't say hey, hi or hello, so Kool didn't feel the need to return the pleasantries.

"A ride to the airport," she told him, bluntly. Farren just wasn't in the mood to be nice or cute. She needed a ride to the airport and that's what it was. Now maybe later, she would feel like flirting or smiling.

What she really desired was a vacation with no cell phones and no children. She just wanted to go to the Bahamas, by herself.

And she planned on doing that as soon as she wrapped up this civil rights case.

"You at your home girl's house?" he asked.

"Yeah," she told him.

"I'll send one of my lil niggas to come scoop you, but next time call your ass an Uber," he said and hung the phone up.

Farren knew Kool was probably feeling she tried him, especially since they hadn't had a real decent conversation since their sexual activities, and the first time they actually did talk, she'd only called for a favor.

Kool can act all nonchalant all he wanted, but she knew he was feeling some type of way and she told herself that she needed to make things right with him. He was a cool ass nigga and it was very rare that you met real men these days.

Farren wasn't planning on taking anything with her. She told herself to check on Jonte, get him and attorney and get back on the plane. She wouldn't be doing the most or putting on her superwoman cape to save anybody because Jonte was grown and he made this decision all by himself.

See the difference with The Cartel is that in situations like this you were protected. If Jonte was in The Cartel he probably wouldn't even have made it to jail, let alone had handcuffs on.

The Cartel had so many policemen and law government officials on their payroll, it was ridiculous. Farren wondered if she was cool with Mr. Bianchi still would he had given her the heads up on Jonte.

Farren hears a car honk outside, so she went to kiss her children and hug Ashley real tight.

"I will be right back, your cousin Kennedy is coming to get y'all in the morning. Michael that money is for you and your sisters not just you, okay?" Farren told her son.

"Yes ma'am, I got you," he told her, fanning through the hundreds.

"Noel, can you play nurse until mommy gets back?" she asked her daughter.

Noel nodded her head, "Auntie Ashley doesn't like to eat, but make sure she eats and takes her medicine. If she doesn't, call me or her boyfriend. Our numbers are right here and they are in Mike's phone," she instructed.

The person who was taking her to the airport, honked again. Farren checked to make sure she had her knife in her purse, she made a mental note to dump it before she went through the security gates at the airport.

Ashley was at the door. "Girl get out of here," she said, coughing.

"I'm coming right back," Farren's eyes pleaded with her to stay alive.

Ashley heard the urgency in her voice. "I'll see you when you get back, text me when you land," she said. Ashley couldn't stand long even with the cane.

Farren told Michael, "Come help auntie get back in the bed," she said and closed the door.

She got in the front seat of the dude's car. "I'm sorry, my best friend has cancer…." she tried to explain for her tardiness.

The nigga didn't even acknowledge her, he just turned the radio up.

Farren was taken back by his rudeness, but she said nothing. Midway through the ride, something stood about him and it was the pinky rings he wore on his left and right hands.

They looked really very familiar, she knew they looked familiar because she had bought those same rings for Christian Knight.

Farren thought she was tripping, but Christian Knight loved custom pieces, nothing he rocked could be found in any jewelry store. She remembered visiting his jeweler often to make sure that these rings were exquisite.

Farren was going to ask Kool about this dude, something raised a red flag and she was ready to get the fuck out of his car.

Once they made it to Hartsfield Jackson Airport, he looked at her and asked, "What airline?" He even had a Jersey accent.

Who was this nigga? Farren thought to herself.

"Delta," she told him, in a very dry tone.

He looked so familiar, but she couldn't place his face at all.

Finally she got out the car and went through security clearance. Farren had to run through the airport because she was about to miss her flight.

Chapter Eight

Farren patiently waited on Jonte to enter the room. She had to go home, shower and put on her corporate attire to get a visit. Farren also had to take his case to get a private visit. Jonte entered the small room looking defeated, but she didn't pity him. It was all of his fault, he dug this hole for himself.

Farren looked over his case and it really was a wrap for him, he was on his third strike. There was no excuse she could possibly come up with for a jury to go easy on him with a lighter sentence.

He sat down at the table, with his arms crossed.

"Don't even waste your time," he told her, watching Farren making notes while going through the folder.

"Oh, I'm glad you already know that I'm not," she told him, matter-of-factly.

"Where are the kids? How is Ashley?" he asked. Jonte didn't want to talk about his fuck ups, he wanted to discuss happier subjects like his children.

"In Atlanta. What are you going to do about Morgan? She cries all day for you," Farren told him.

"That's all I been thinking about, my baby girls and Mike. Man, I fucked up," he said, wiping tears from his face.

Farren's tone softened, she had only seen him cry once and that was when his brother died.

He was hurting.

"I can bring her to visit you," Farren told him.

He shook his head, "It's only going to make things worse," he said.

"Jonte, what do you want me to do then? She asked.

"I'll let you know. I'll call Mike's phone today and talk to her," he said.

"I need a favor though," he asked.

She raised her eyebrow. "I need you to make sure Spider and Mari get out," he said.

"And what about Trina?" Farren asked, only to be sarcastic.

"Don't worry about that," he brushed her off.

"I'll get on it. Did they offer you a deal yet?" she questioned.

"Yeah, I didn't take it. I'm taking the fall for everything. They need to be released soon before Mari start feeling the pressure and running her damn mouth," he whispered.

"I'm getting her out, but that's it. I don't fuck with her," she told Jonte.

"Just write her another check…for me. Please?" he asked.

Farren was wondering what kind of damn voodoo Mari ran on Jonte. He had really been defensive about Mari lately and it was starting to get on her damn nerves.

"I'm moving to Atlanta," she told him.

"For real?" he asked.

She nodded. "I'll see if I can get you transported there," she promised him.

Farren had a few connects in the office still from when she was running shit back in the day with Christian Knight by her side.

"Kiss the kids for me. Are you mad at me?" he asked.

"Not at all, just hate that the kids don't have you anymore, you know you were their favorite," she teased.

That made Jonte laugh, he needed to laugh.

"Do you need anything?" she asked him. Farren was already planning on reach out to Mario to ask for protection while he was in there.

"Nah, I'm good. You can drop some money in the account and all that when you get a chance, I'm not pressed," he told her. Jail didn't change Jonte, he was still super laid back and cool.

"I hate this happened to you," she told him, sincerely.

"Life is one big gamble, baby," he told her.

She rubbed his hand and he reached down and kissed hers.

Farren took a deep breath once they came and removed Jonte from the room. Five years ago she would have never thought that she would be visiting him in jail, especially after they had countless conversations about him being over the street life and wanting to do something with himself. Farren took a lot of time out of her very busy schedule to show him how to run a plethora of successful businesses.

She didn't know when it got boring to him.

Although, Jonte was grown, she still blamed Mari.

Farren left the jail with her spirit down just a lil bit.

She went to one of her favorite dessert spots, ordered a slice of caramel cheesecake and a glass of water with lemon.

She pulled out her favorite notepad, and made a few notes in relations to her moving to Atlanta. She was going to go put some fresh flowers on Christian's grave, pack her house up and sell it. She was going to increase the manger's salaries of the businesses that Jonte opened and would just collect monthly on them. Farren refused to sell her condo in New York, it held entirely too many memories for her.

She needed to transfer the kids' schools before the summer ended, and last but not least, try to convince her mom to either move to Houston with Neeki or to Atlanta with her. Farren's mama really needed to leave Hardy alone, wasn't shit going on there at all.

Kim called her and Farren knew she had been ignoring her for too long. "Farren, I miss you," she told her, truthfully.

"I miss you too, I'm sorry. I've just been taking care of my kids," she admitted.

Farren went ghost from everything and everybody, she was just really focused right now.

"Let's link soon. I was just calling to see if you were going to pick up," she told her.

Farren laughed. "See, don't give up on me! I answered," she told her.

"You shole right about that. Okay boo, I'll be in touch," Kim told her.

Farren took her time, enjoying her water and dessert. So much had happened this year, she was ready for January 1st already.

Farren called Kool. "Yo," he answered.

"I made it safe," she told him.

"That's wasup," he said.

"The dude who came and got me, what's his name?" she inquired.

"Why? You want me to put you on," he asked, jealous.

"Boy please. No, I feel like I've seen him before," she told him.

"Well he's my cousin, we probably favor," he said.

"Nah, somewhere else. In New York," Farren said.

"His mama, my auntie, is from New York, but he and his girl had moved here a few years ago," he said.

"What's his girl name? That's probably how I know him," Farren said.

"Asia, I doubted if you know her," he said.

Farren dropped her knife. "Ohh okay. Nah, I don't know her," she lied.

"Yeah, she's way younger than you," Kool said.

"How long has he been in the A?" Farren questioned.

"About three years, I told him to come down here and get some money with me," he said.

"Hmm hmm, well let me go. I'm wrapping up loose ends up here. Are you going to come get me from the airport?" Farren asked, sweetly.

"You're bipolar," he said.

"No, I'm not. I'm just not into wasting my time or playing games."

"Whatever, just text me before you get on your flight," he said and hung up the phone. That nigga Kool was extremely too rude in her opinion.

Farren didn't feel like packing up and all that, she went home and took a nap. In the morning, she would be going to her law firm to get Mari and Spider the best attorney she could. She was going to give them the retainer and head back to Atlanta.

Farren called her mom as she drove home, "What it do?" her mom answered.

Farren couldn't do anything but laugh, her mother didn't age at all.

"Nothing, just left from seeing Jonte," she said.

"How is he doing?" her mother asked, genuinely concerned.

"Good, he already know what it is," she told him.

"Sho nuff. How's Ashley doing?"

"She's okay, she just look real tired, super tired."

"That's how your daddy was girl," her mama said.

Farren got a little sad at the mentioning of her father, she missed him so much along with Dice and Christian.

"Ma, I'm moving to Atlanta," she said.

"Aww baby, I can see you living there, ain't nothing for you here in Jersey," she said, spitting out some tobacco.

"Uh ain't nothing for you here either. Move with me? I'll get you a house so you can have your own space," she said.

Her mother quickly said, "Nah, I'm good."

"Ma why? I'm not leaving you in no raggedy Hardy."

"Farren, I like where I live, I like playing poker when I get off work, and I like my job. I don't wanna move," she told her daughter.

Farren couldn't do nothing but shake her head. "Are you sure?"

"Real sure. I've been living out here since I was a little girl, my mama grew up out here and my grandmother," she said.

Farren didn't understand how her mother didn't want to experience life somewhere else it was almost as if she refused.

"Alright ma," she said.

"Love you, baby. I'm about to back outside, call me later," she said.

Farren prayed for her mama's safety, she was going to put some money in her account before she headed to the airport tomorrow.

Farren didn't get any sleep, her mind was consumed with so much. The only thing that she was excited about was her move to Atlanta. She just wanted to be surrounding by something new, new food, new locations, and new people. Shit, new everything. Jersey didn't have anything to offer her but sad memories. Farren was up before the sun, she took a warm bubble bath and made herself a cup of coffee with some coffee beans that she purchased on the last vacation she took with Jonte. She planned on writing him a very long letter once he got to wherever he was going, but she was going to try to get him transferred to Atlanta. Farren boxed up some clothes for her and the kids and dropped them off at the post office, so they could be at Ashley's house by the end of the week.

She made her way to the law office she had recently started working at, she asked one of the defense attorneys to take the case.

"Are you sure you don't wanna take it?" Timothy asked her.

"Nah, I'm good. My friend is sick, I don't have the time," she told him. She left him a blank check. "Just text me with the amount you fill it out for, but whatever the price is, I'm cool with," she told him.

Timothy had heard how Farren Knight used to be a beast a few years back in the courtroom, he heard that she was pretty rich as well.

"What made you choose me?" he asked, out of curiosity.

"You remind me of me back in the day, hungry for success. First one here, last one to leave, trust me it pays off in the end," she told him with a big smile.

"'Text me if you need me," she told him, and exited his office.

Farren parked her car at her condo and caught a cab to the airport. She was ready to head back to the South, she was missing her spoiled ass kids and she knew she needed to rush back to Atlanta.

Kool picked her up from the airport as promised, and took her to dinner at Houston's.

"You like me?" Kool asked.

Farren rolled her eyes. Why was she always getting stuck with the niggas who had the tough exterior, but were secretly super mushy and emotional? She really needed to be done with hood niggas, for real.

Farren wondered if a lawyer or a doctor could fuck her as good as a hood nigga could, she thought about it…Nah.

"Yes I do, but right now…"

Kool threw his hand up. "Don't give me no bullshit, just say yeah you do. That's all I asked for," he told her.

Kool was so controlling that shit turned her on in ways that she couldn't explain.

"I need to tell you something," she told him.

"Tell me later," he told her.

All he wanted was to enjoy his first date. He didn't tell her that he went and got a haircut, and bought some new Bond cologne just to hear her say, "Damn, you smell good," which is what she said as soon as she got in the car at airport curbside pickup.

Kool popped tags on his outfit for tonight too, he knew Farren was in a league all on her own and he had to step it up if he wanted to lock her down.

"So why did you go back up top?" he asked.

"Jonte, my baby daddy got locked up," she told him.

Kool noticed that she didn't sound sad. "You good?" he asked.

"Yeah I am, he's going to be okay."

"When is he coming home?" Kool questioned.

He wasn't into being a side nigga, or something temporary while she was in Atlanta seeing about her home girl.

Kool played bitches all the time, he would be damned if he got played too.

"Never, it was his third strike and he took the rap for a few other folks," she said.

Kool nodded, that was a real nigga move and he saluted dude.

"Damn," was all he said back.

Farren wanted to change the subject. "I'm moving here," she informed him

He couldn't even contain his excitement, and Farren thought it was so cute that he tried to kick it like he didn't care.

"Where bout?" he asked.

"I'm not sure yet." She swallowed a small piece of her salmon.

"That's wasup," he said.

"Who have you been fucking?" she asked. Farren had been wanting to ask him that for the longest.

Kool laughed, "Why?"

"Because I wanna know."

"You must want some more?"

She reached over the table and whispered, "Maybe."

"Yes or no," he commanded.

Farren felt her pussy pulsating, she nodded her head to answer her question.

"Nah, I don't know what that means."

"Yes," she told him with a smirk.

"Check please," he joked.

Farren laughed, this nigga was crazy.

Their food hadn't been on the table for more than five minutes before he asked her if she wanted some dick.

Once the waiter returned to the table and asked how they were doing and how the food tasted, Kool was asking for the check and two to-go plates.

She couldn't stop laughing. "You keep on laughing, I'm about to tear your ass up," he told her, fishing through his wad of money to get the right amount to cover their food and a tip.

Farren checked on the kids and told Kennedy she was going to get them in the morning. Farren made a mental note to Google a company that would drive all of her cars here for her, she might have to pay to get them flew here.

Farren spoke with Ashley's fiancé briefly, he said that Ashely had a good day today and was now sleeping. She was sad because she wanted to speak with her and tell her that she loved her, but she would see her tomorrow.

She then reached out to Timothy to check on Mari and Spider. He told her that by the end of the week they would be home, which was cool for her.

Mari's trifling ass needed to sit in jail and starve

Farren forgot to tell Kennedy to tell Michael to look out for an unknown number to be calling, which would be Jonte.

"How is your friend doing?" Kool asked, once she finished up all her phone calls.

"She's doing well. Her boyfriend just told me that she's in good spirits today," she said with a smile.

"I lost my grandmother recently, so I'm here for you boo," Kool told her rubbing her thigh.

"Thank you, thank you so much," she told him with a smile.

She was about to unzip his pants, she was so damn horny.

UNKNOWN flashed on her cell phone.

"This is him, give me a few minutes," Farren told Kool.

She felt bad about having a full-blown conversation with Jonte after they just had a very nice date and was damn sure about to enjoy their night together.

Kool told her, "Man answer the phone. I'm not lame like that."

Farren had been honest about her relationship with Jonte prior to him getting locked up, so he already knew what it was. Until she gave him a reason to not trust her word, she was 100 in his eyes until further notice.

"Hi," Farren answered.

"Wasup, Mike not answering. Can you call them?" he said getting straight to the point.

She told him to hold on, and she called Kennedy's phone because Mike probably didn't even have that phone near him.

Two minutes later, Morgan was on the phone sounding so delighted to talk to her daddy.

"Daddy!!!!!!!!! I miss you daddy so much," she told her daddy.

Farren heard Jonte's voice cracking, those kids were his weak spots.

Jonte had always had love for his nieces and nephews but the love he had for Carren, Noel, Michael and Morgan was indescribable.

"I miss you too baby girl" he told her.

"When are you coming to get me?" she asked.

"Mommy is going to bring you to me in a few days," he promised.

"Aww no, I want you now," she cried.

"Morgan stop. Now listen, you gotta be a big girl for mommy," he told her.

Farren heard Noel fussing in the background saying she wanted to talk to him.

Farren spoke up, "Morgan give the phone to Noel"

Morgan screamed, 'no"

Jonte intervened, "let me talk to Noel for a lil second Morgan" he pleaded.

Noel finally was able to get the phone out of Morgan's little hands. "Hey daddy, Morgan is getting on my nerves, and mama don't beat her," she said in one breath.

Farren shook her head, Noel didn't know her mama was on the phone.

Jonte laughed. "You just worry about you, I miss you boonk," he told her.

"I miss you too. What's going on?" she asked.

"Nothing, y'all will see me soon and I will tell you. Let me talk to Mike real quick," he said, once the operator said it was only sixty seconds remaining.

"What up Jonte?" his baby deep voice boomed over the phone.

"Hey put your phone on loud, I'ma try and call back in an hour, and it's an unknown number. I need to talk to you, so don't tell your sisters it's me on the phone," he told him.

"Okay I got you. Love you," he said.

Farren had never heard her son tell Jonte he loved him, but it did warm her heart.

"Love you too," he told him.

"Farren?" he called her name out once they all hung up.

"Yes"

"Love you, I'll call you tomorrow. Be safe," he said.

"Okay. I love you too and it's handled," she told him, referring to Mari and Spider.

"Good looking out," he said and they ended the call.

Kool made a left then a right into his subdivision, she would have never guessed that his hood ass would have such a nice home.

It was perfect for him.

"I love this couch," Farren squealed.

"My sister hooked me up, I don't really come here that much. I got a lil spot in the hood, but I knew that I couldn't take you there," he told her, cutting the lights on.

"And why not?" she asked.

"I fuck hoes there," he told her, keeping it real.

"So who gets to come here?" she questioned.

"Family on holidays," he told her, honestly.

Farren made herself comfortable on his couch, it was so lavish and player. She would be asking Kool to ask his sister where she purchased all of his living room furniture.

Kool joined her on the couch with a beer and some weed and a pack of rolling papers.

"You were supposed to offer me something to drink," she told him, laughing and getting up to find her way to his kitchen to make her a drink.

"I'm a hood nigga, baby. What's mine is yours, so make yourself comfortable," he told her.

Farren really liked his house, it was so nice.

She fixed her a small cup of Hennessy. She didn't normally drink brown, but that was all he had.

"What you wanna watch?" he asked Farren once she returned to the living room.

She laid her feet in his lap and flexed her toes.

"Damn, you got some pretty feet," he told her

"Kiss em." She brought her foot to his mouth.

Kool laid back. "Nah, I don't do feet," he told her.

"You do mine," she told him, teasing him.

Kool handed her the remote and took her feet in his feet and started rubbing them.

Farren cut the television off and got comfortable. "What are your flaws?" she asked.

She just wanted to get to know him.

"Huh?" he asked.

"What don't you like about you? What do you wish to change about yourself?" she questioned. The problem with people these days is that no one stopped to ask questions. Females laid down with whoever because he was cute, or his car was nice, or he got a lil money. You can't fuck everybody.

Conversations were so limited these days, then people wondered why their relationships don't last, because y'all weren't compatible to begin with.

Kool took a pull on his blunt. He handed it to her, but she told him no. Farren wasn't in the mood to smoke.

"I don't know. I need to learn balance when I'm grinding, I don't wanna be bothered," he said.

"What else?" she fished for more information.

"Uhh, I don't have any patience. I don't do girlfriends. I'm to myself, I'm real quiet and I don't like conversations like these," he said laughing.

Farren was putting him on the spot and he didn't know how to answer her questions.

"So that's what we about to be doing? Just fucking?" she asked.

"Well, being that you just got out of a relationship and you just buried your husband or whatever he was to you, yeah for now," he told her straight up.

Kool didn't understand how she was comfortable to be jumping into another relationship so soon, like he wondered was she sad. Was her feelings hurt, was she even healed from the funeral. He wasn't into being somebody' down time.

He actually liked Farren, so he planned on taking his time with her.

"You're right. I agree with you 100%, I'm just making sure we're on the same page," she told him.

He didn't respond, just continued smoking his Kush and rubbing her toes with his other hand.

Farren stared at him as she laid propped up on a few pillows.

"Your cousin set my husband up," she told him.

He looked at her, "Say what?" he asked.

"Kiss and his girlfriend. I lied when I told you I didn't know who Asia was, I know exactly who she is," Farren told him.

"Well, why lie?" he asked.

"Because I had to think first."

"Think about what?" Kool was on Farren's ass like white on rice.

"Look, don't come at me like that." She sat up.

"Come at you like what shawty? I got this nigga around my money and my work. You think Bianchi wanna hear about a fuck up in case some shit go down? If he's a snake, then I need to know," he roared.

Farren regretted even saying anything, but she knew she had to continue.

"Those pinky rings he wears, I bought those for Christian." She picked up her cell phone off the coffee table and found the picture of her and Christian Knight caked up in the strip club one night.

Kool zoomed in one the pictures and yeah the pinky rings were identical, but he wasn't about to go fucking with his cousin on this little bit of evidence.

"What else?" he asked, rubbing his hands over his fade.

"What you mean what else?"

"How do you know Asia?" he asked.

"Uhh let me think… She took my husband from me, they were fucking around for years! When your sorry ass cousin got out of jail, he convinced her to set him up," Farren was getting frustrated.

"Let's ride," he told her, hopping up.

"Ride where?" she asked.

"No questions."

"Okay, just forewarning you. I know how to use my gun very, very well and I will not hesitate to shoot you," she told him in a very serious tone.

"Damn, it's like that?" Kool asked.

"Yeah, I don't know where I'm going, so it's definitely like that," Farren answered his question.

"Just ride shawty." He opened the garage door and Farren followed him to his car.

The entire ride was quiet. Kool played music, but he wasn't listening to it and neither was she.

They pulled up to a popular strip club in Atlanta called Onyx.

Kool paid for them to skip their line and she followed him closely to a section that was filled with niggas, apparently his niggas.

Kool didn't introduce her because he didn't like people in his business, he only came to observe Kiss around Farren.

After he spoke to his crew, he pulled Farren close to him and acted as if he was kicking some smooth shit to her, "I'ma go get us a bottle, just stay on your phone and play this shit cool," he told her.

Farren knew what he was saying without him saying much, so she took a seat; game face on and all.

She texted Kim and her sister in a group message, asking for a trip to the spa soon.

She felt someone's cold stare on her and lo and behold it was that nigga Kiss. Farren stared right back at his ass, he broke out in a laugh and returned to his attention back to the strippers they had paid to stay in their section for the remainder of the night.

Kool had peeped it all. About an hour and a half later, one of the niggas in their crew said, "Let's take these hoes back to the trap."

The rest of the dudes agreed. "Boss, you sliding through?" they asked Kool.

Kool looked over at Farren, she already knew what to say. "I want to go home," she whined.

"Nah, I'ma pass y'all. Shawty is tired," he said.

A few minutes later, they all left in one big multitude. Kool went the opposite way of them since the rest of the crew were trailing each other.

"What are you going to do?" she asked him.

Farren wasn't nervous. She had seen enough of crazy stuff working for The Cartel, her stomach could handle anything at this point.

"Kill his ass," he said, nonchalantly.

"Your cousin?" she asked to be sure.

Farren didn't like heartless niggas, but for Kool it was about respect and most importantly loyalty.

He couldn't break bread with a nigga that came up by stepping on another man's head. That's just not how Kool rocked. Everything he got, he worked hard as hell for it and would be damned if another man took from him especially he when he least expected it.

Kool ignored her, he pulled on a side street.

"You coming in?" he asked.

"No," she told him.

"Man get out," he told her.

Farren smacked her lips and got out the car.

They walked around the corner to a small house, but it was so many cars lined up and down the street.

Kool knocked. "Man, I thought you wasn't coming," one of the lil young bucks said, once he unlocked the door.

Farren made a mental note of everyone in the room, she saw that it was guns everywhere, this was a real trap.

She hadn't been in a trap since Dice was living.

Farren was feeling a lil Hollywood in the place, her face was super frowned up.

"Where is Kiss?" Kool asked.

"In the kitchen," someone told him.

Kool pulled out his gun and everybody got quiet. Kool went to the kitchen, Kiss was standing over the counter rolling a blunt.

He looked up and saw Kool standing there with his gun by his side.

"Wasup cuz?" he asked. Kiss wasn't nervous or nothing, he was a hood nigga to the fullest and ain't never feared death a day in his life.

"Come here," Kool told him.

"For what?" he asked, finishing up stuffing his blunt.

"Man, I ain't got all day," Kool told him.

"Okay cuz," he told him, lighting the blunt.

Kiss walked straight pass him and went to the living room. He was mad as fuck that he didn't have his pistol on him.

He went to grab one on the floor, but Farren kicked it out the way.

"Bitch," Kiss mumbled.

"Aye say cuz, you know my girl?" Kool asked.

Everyone just sat in silence, trying to see what the fuck was going on.

"Yeah, I think so," he said.

"She say you robbed her husband and set him up, that's where you got that work from?" Kool questioned.

Kiss nodded, "And what? This your hoe or something cuz? You got your gun out like you wanna do something?" he boasted.

"Man, do you know who I'm rocking with right now? If they find the shit out it makes me look like a snake cus you my family," he told Kiss.

"And what? We're blood," he yelled.

"I can't let you fuck my money up," he told him.

Kool shot at his head, but missed. Kool looked at him "You about to kill me? I shared a bed with you, really nigga!" he shouted and came at Kool.

"You wanna fight? Come on now, me and you both now you're not no fighter," Kool chuckled.

"Let's go. Squad up," Kiss told him, getting in a fighting stance.

Kool didn't have time to be wrestling with this nigga, he shot him twice and his body dropped instantly.

No one in the trap muttered one word. Kool looked over at the hoes that was present, and his crew already knew without him saying anything that the girls had to die tonight. He was sure that they were going to fuck the shit out of them before ending their lives. He didn't care what they did with them, they shouldn't have been at a trap house at four in the morning anyway, trying to get wifed up. What nigga wanted a girl in a trap house? If a woman didn't have respect for herself, then how could she expect a nigga to have respect for her?

"Clean this shit up, and this should warn y'all niggas, blood or not. I am not the one to play with," Kool said real calmly. He raised his Givenchy t-shirt up and wiped the blood off of his face.

Farren reached down and took the pinky rings off of him.

"I bought those for my husband," she said.

She wouldn't cry in front of all of these niggas, but when she got in the car she probably would.

Although death was nothing to be happy about, she felt good knowing that the earth was free from one pussy nigga. Only thing was, there were a million more left.

Kool opened the door for her and they walked quickly to the car.

He had to burn his clothes ASAP.

"The Cartel will handle that for you," she told him.

"I handled it. I don't need them in my business," he said.

"Are you okay?" she asked.

"Yeah bae, I'm good," he told her.

His adrenaline was racing, now he wanted some pussy.

Kool reached his hand between Farren's legs and moved her thong to the side. "Damn, you're wet as fuck," he told her.

She slid down in her seat to give him better access as he finger fucked her so good.

Kool did 120 on the highway trying to get home.

"Hmm yessss," Farren moaned.

He really didn't even want to wait until he got home, his dick was hard as hell.

Kool pulled over on the highway. "Get out," he told her, unlocking the door.

"Huh? What? I don't like outside," Farren whined.

"Come on, turn up with me one time," Kool told her, offering her a very warm smile.

Farren slid her thong off, Kool lifted his console and placed a condom on his dick.

The wind was blowing and Farren was cold. She had never done anything like this and she was too damn old to be fucking on the side of the highway.

Kool opened her door and told her to bend over and place her face in the seat, he crouched real low and stuck his dick deep off in her guts.

"Oh my!" Farren took a deep breath, she wasn't expecting it to feel like that. It was all in her, she couldn't fathom the feeling her body was experiencing. Kool knew that they had all night to be passionate, for now he was trying to bust this nut so they could get home safe. At the rate he was going, they were going to crash.

"Throw that shit back," Kool told her, smacking her ass.

He damn near climbed on top of her, trying to get balls deep off in that pussy.

Kool increased his strokes and Farren had tears coming out of her eyes, it felt so good.

There was no way this little quiet man had her feeling so blissful.

She was moaning so loud, anyone who passed by on the highway with their window down and were driving in complete silence, definitely heard her moaning and yelling for Kool to fuck her harder.

"I'm about to nut," Kool whispered.

"Hmm, cum with me baby," she told him, throwing it back and twerking on his dick, making his stomach way more wetter and stickier.

Farren's juices were everywhere. "I'm cumming Kool. Oh my God," she moaned.

And together they came, high off of good sex and murder.

He laid on top of her, trying to regain a steady heartbeat.

"Get off of me, you're heavy," Farren told him, half-joking and telling the truth at the same time.

"Girl hush," he told her.

Kool stretched, he threw the condom out in the woods and pulled his jeans back up, he knew he had fucked his sneakers up, but that nut was worth it.

"What's your real name?" she asked.

"Karter," he told her.

"Wow," she said sadly.

"What?" he questioned.

"I had a miscarriage and we were planning on naming my son Carter, that's all."

He reached over and kissed her passionately.

"Don't fuck over me, cus I'll kill you," he told her.

Farren saw the seriousness in his eyes and it made her want to just cling to him.

But she knew she needed to get her mind together before she began yet another relationship.

She kissed him back, but said nothing.

Kool pulled off of the median and back onto the highway.

Farren danced in her seat, she loved the music that the radio station in Atlanta played. Half of the time she didn't know what the young rappers were saying, but nevertheless she enjoyed the beat.

"You good?" Kool asked, he had never seen Farren so loose and happy.

She was either crying or mad about something, which is one reason why Kool really wanted them to take their time getting to know each other because he felt like they didn't really know each other. He had just told her his real name, although he was sure it was in his file, unless she just was trying to put her time with The Cartel behind her.

"That back there was good," she told him, still dancing.

"Yeah it was, you got a fire hydrant between your legs," Kool complimented told her.

Farren didn't respond, the wind was feeling so good outside on her sticky sweaty skin and the music was jamming and she was riding with a real nigga.

Although, she had buried her estranged husband and her father this year, risked her life for a multi-billionaire illegal organization, damn near got dragged out of a massive estate in Miami, Florida along with visiting her baby-daddy and ex-fiancé in jail where he would be for the rest of his life. Oh and let's not forget her best friend was diagnosed with stomach cancer.

Farren refused to complain, besides all of that. Life was okay.

She would be okay. Once she learned to accept things for what they were.

They were a little tired, once they made it back to this house. They showered quickly, Kool was knocked out before Farren could dry off and put on one of his t-shirts.

She was confused and didn't know what she was doing. Farren knew that she wanted to leave Jersey, but she knew that law wasn't her passion; it was a paycheck.

Farren needed to get her head on tight, she needed to focus and prioritize. It pained her to admit that she didn't like being alone.

Sleep found her before she found it. Drowning in her own misery, silently crying for happiness, for contentment, but most importantly, stability, she drifted off to sleep.

Farren didn't know how long she was knocked out, but she really needed that sleep.

"Your phone keep ringing," Kool nudged her softly. He stood over her shirtless looking good enough to fuck all over again.

Farren wiped the slob from the side of her mouth, and took the phone from her hands.

The voice on the other line, delivered news that although she knew it would come one day. She was dreading and didn't expect it to be *today*.

Chapter Nine

Farren packed up Ashley's things and placed the last of her bathroom stuff in a box, she refused to attend any more funerals this year. Farren told her mother, she didn't have any more strength to witness someone that she loved get buried six feet under. She just refused to go through this again. Farren asked God the day of the funeral to comfort her and bring her peace. Her heart was aching for her best friend. Someone who had always had her back no matter what, wrong or right, Ashley had been there. There wasn't a jealous bone in her body nor did Farren never have to question her loyalty. Ashley was that friend, the kind of friend that African-American woman secretly prayed for. The friend that was always there when you wanted her to be and even when you didn't. The friend that listened and still offered her opinion whether you asked for it not. The friend that didn't miss anything you had going on. Ashley was an amazing woman who lost the battle of life to cancer. She knew she was in a better place and for that reason only was she able to not be angry, but to attempt to move on with her life because that's what Ashley would want her to do.

"Is this everything?" Kool asked.

Farren had decided to donate all of Ashley's things to a younger woman with four children that Kool knew in the neighborhood that he grew up in. Kitchen, living room, bedroom furniture and everything, the young woman would be definitely surprised to receive such good quality things.

"Yeah, just about," Farren told him wiping the sweat from for her forehead, today was a real workout.

Ashley's boyfriend wasn't much help, he stayed in her closet the majority of the day.

Farren went to tell him goodbye before her and Kool departed.

"Hey, I'm about to leave. Are you going to be okay?" she asked.

He wiped his face. "I can't live without her. Do you know I begged Ashley to marry me and she always told me no? She was scared of commitment," he said.

Farren remained silent, Ashley always kicked it like as if them not marrying after all these years was a mutual agreement.

"What is life without Ashley?" he asked.

Farren took a deep breath. "I just buried my husband not too long ago, so trust me I know how you feel. I know what you're going through, but time heals all wounds. Take some time for yourself, don't rush back to work. Go on vacation, read a book. Ashley doesn't want you crying," Farren told him.

He nodded his head. "I'll be okay," he told her.

Farren knew that he was lying, she had been in his shoes before. Death was a very hard pill to swallow, especially when it's your significant other.

"Bae," Kool called her name.

"I'm about to leave, I'll lock the front door," Farren told him.

He didn't respond, so she exited quietly.

Once they got in the car and Kool made sure the U-Haul was closed securely. They pulled off.

Unbeknownst to Farren, Ashley's fiancé put a bullet through his head less than five minutes after they exited.

"So when are you coming back?" Kool asked, once he brought Farren to the airport.

"Few days, I just gotta wrap up some loose ends. Why?" she asked.

"Just asking boo, I be missing you," Kool said. He had been trying his hardest to keep his feelings in check, but women like Farren didn't come around every day and he would be doing some serious lying if he said he wasn't becoming smitten of her.

In just a very short period of time, Farren had sunk her claws into his heart. Kool had been dodging all his bitches and even heading over to Ashley's house early instead of hanging in the trap all night.

"Aww babe, I'll be back soon. I gotta go get the kids, make sure my house is together for when people stop by to check it out. Hopefully it sells soon," she told him.

Farren had found a nice four bedroom house out in Smyrna, Georgia and she couldn't wait to return to Georgia so she could began decorating. What made her even happier was that the kids were just as excited about the move as well. All Noel asked for was that her mommy find her a soccer team to play for and Michael just wanted a house with a basement, so he could play the game in silence.

Farren planned on doing a little real estate while working on her next book and whatever else came to mind.

"Fa sho, be safe and hit my line when you land," he told her.

They kissed briefly, one thing Farren appreciated about Kool was that he was a very private man. He wasn't big on public displays of affection which was perfect with her because she wasn't either. There was nothing wrong with holding hands now and then, but doing the most in public wasn't something that Farren wasn't fond of. She believed that discretion was always key, and that was with anything that she involved herself in. Farren didn't believe in posting every meal, drink, shopping spree or vacation. Somethings were meant to savor for you and you only that was just her outlook on life.

Farren hopped out of his truck and headed in the airport. Surprisingly, the person that randomly had crossed her mind was calling her phone.

"Hello?"

"Mrs. Knight, how are you?" Mario, Farren's friend asked once she answered the phone.

"I'm well stranger, and you?" she asked.

"Stranger? Nah just been busy. When are you coming my way again?" he questioned.

"No time soon, my last visit there wasn't too pleasant," Farren said, her voice drifted when she thought of the horrid way that Jeff had passed.

Farren hated Miami.

"Too bad to hear that, but I'm pretty sure you'll be back soon," Mario told her.

"Don't hold your breath boo" she told him, going through security clearance.

"Mario, let me call you back I'm in the airport, service going in and out" she told him.

"No problem take care love" he told her and disconnected the call.

Farren was happy that her friend thought about her and called to see how she was doing, it made her day.

After arriving in New Jersey, Farren went to get her kids from her mom's house, they had flew back with her after the funeral.

"That chile been crying for her daddy all day, I had to sit her lil ass on the balcony and cut my music on," Farren's mom told her, once she made it to her apartment.

"I know, she's missing her daddy. I'm going to see if I can arrange a visit before we leave," Farren told her mom.

She had been working really hard to get him transferred down south, really Atlanta, Georgia, but if not at least somewhere close.

"Those visits are only makes things worse if you ask me."

"Well ma, that's the only solution I have right now," she snapped. Her mama was cool and all, but she always gave her opinion at the wrong time.

"Okay baby. I just think that a twenty or thirty minute visit is only going to confuse her even more. Have you told Noel and Michael?" she asked.

Farren rolled her eyes, these were her kids and she didn't want or need any help raising her children.

"Jonte spoke with both of them. Look ma, I'm about to go. I got a lot to do and I'm tired," she said, calling the children to the front room.

Nakia knew when her opinion wasn't considered, so she kept her mouth shut.

Farren gathered her kids and took them home, the entire ride Morgan kept asking was her daddy home. Farren was tired and very frustrated, she had a lot to get done and her daughter's constant whining and crying really wasn't making things better for her at all. Farren said, "Morgan please stop crying and screaming. You are giving mommy a headache. Okay? I am tired, I am very tired. I have been cleaning out your auntie's house out all day," she said, putting her hand on her head.

"I WANT MY DADDY!" Morgan screamed and kicked the back of Farren's chair.

She tried her hardest to keep calm and maintain her composure, she really did. Farren was angry, she was bitter, she felt empty. Her best friend was gone and it suddenly hit her that she was running to Atlanta, but Ashley wasn't in Atlanta.

"CALL MY DADDY!" Morgan kicked the chair and cried.

Farren had enough, she was officially fed the fuck up. Her truck swerved from the left lane all the way to the right and she pulled over in the nearest gas station parking lot and drove to the back.

"Give me your belt!" she yelled at Mike.

He hurriedly took it off and handed it to his mama. "Bout time," he mumbled under his breath.

He had been wanting to tap lil Morgan's behind, a time or two. She cried all day every day and it was annoying.

Farren unbuckled her seatbelt, snatched Morgan's lil ass out of her booster seat and tore her to pieces.

"Listen to me lil girl, your daddy is not at home, and he's not coming home. He will never tuck you in again or watch Frozen with you again in his life. Do you hear me?" she yelled.

Morgan's heart broke into tiny pieces when she heard the news, she didn't understand what her mom was saying to her. Morgan was a daddy's girl to the fullest. Farren knew she was too young to understand what jail was so she didn't even bother with that conversation, it was pointless.

"I will bathe you, put you to bed, kiss your boo-boos and watch *Frozen* all day every day with you," she told her.

"But all that crying is going to stop, every time you cry I'ma beat you down," she threatened her and she meant it.

Morgan instantly sucked all those tears up, and got back in her car seat.

"Y'all good? Y'all want a whooping too?" she asked her other two kids.

They both shook their heads no.

"That's what I thought," she said, and started the truck back up and resumed their journey home.

Eleven days, and more than a million trips to the Post Office later, it was the Knight Family's last day in Jersey, not forever but for the summer at least. Farren was a Jersey girl at heart. She was quite sure that they would be visiting often, especially since her mom still lived here and the kids had friends here they really wanted to keep in touch with.

"We're going to the airport this early?" Mike yawned, from the front seat.

"No, today is a busy day for us. First, we're going to breakfast then we are going to see Jonte," she said.

Noel erupted into happiness, she was so ecstatic to hear that.

"Then we are going to go see y'all other grandmother, since she's in the nursing home, then we're going to go say goodbye to daddy and Carren," she told her kids.

"I don't wanna go there," Mike said, sadly.

"You can stay in the car baby," she told him, rubbing her hands on the top of his head.

Farren had to say goodbye to her loved ones. She couldn't move to a whole other region without leaving fresh flowers on Carren's grave.

The family made their way to the correctional facility where Jonte was being held, Farren arranged a personal visit, but this time the ticket price was a thousand dollars.

"Daddy!!!!!!!!!" Morgan ran to Jonte's arms.

Jonte picked her up and span her around, she was so happy to see him, Noel and Michael was too.

Farren allowed the kids to ask him a million questions about his stay here, which Jonte kept sugarcoating.

Morgan whispered in her daddy's ear and Jonte's face frowned up. "You whooped her?" he asked.

"Do not start with me," she told him.

"Why did you whoop her?" he questioned.

"Because she was getting on my nerves," Farren told him.

"Don't do that shit again," he warned. Farren wanted to say, "And nigga if I did, what were you going to do", but she kept her mouth shut and allowed the kids to enjoy their time with the man that they came to know as "Dad".

"How are you?" he asked her.

"I'm tired, just trying to keep everything afloat," she told him.

"You look tired, take you a vacation man. Don't let this life eat you away," he told her.

Jonte was always so chill and laid-back, never allowing anything to take him out of his natural element of serenity and peace.

"I'll think about it," she told him.

"You talked to Mari?" he asked.

"Uh no, you think that she would have called to say thank you for getting me out," Farren spat.

Jonte shook his head. "Go by there and tell her y'all moving," he said.

"For what? I don't want her in my business," she told Jonte.

"You know she love these kids, don't even act like that," Jonte scolded Farren.

"Y'all wanna say bye to Auntie Mari?" Jonte asked.

Of course, like little Jonte robots they all screamed, "Yes!"

Farren rolled her eyes, she wasn't stunting Mari's ass and if Mari loved the kids so much she damn sure hadn't offered to babysit in a while.

"I love y'all so much, Morgan be good for your mama," Jonte told his baby girl.

Farren stood and hugged Jonte tight. "Keep your head up in here boy, it's plenty of money on your books. You call me if something goes wrong."

"Look at you, trying to see about me. I'm good bae," he said smiling.

Jonte still had that D-Boy charm about him that Farren loved so much. Jail or no jail, Jonte was still sexy as hell. Farren had to bite her lip just thinking about all of the love that they used to make.

Jonte was that nigga who didn't care if you was having a bad day and just wanted to come home, take a shower and go to sleep. If he wanted some pussy, oh you'd better believe your ass was about to spread them legs and give it to him. Farren's mind took her back to one night when he came home late drunk and high. The kids had drove her fucking crazy and once they finally fell asleep, she was super happy.

"Move," she told him in her sleep.

But Jonte wasn't trying to hear none of that, he came home with his girl's pussy on his mind and that's what he planned on getting.

"I miss you," Jonte climbed on top of her and planted sweet kisses on her neck.

He lifted her pajama shirt and started kissing all on her chest and fingering her nipples with his hands.

"Jonte, I had a real long day," she whined and squirmed trying to get from under him.

"Just let me slide it in," he whispered. Farren rolled her eyes that was a nigga favorite line and in three minutes or less, they had you in a million different positions.

Farren knew she had to give him what he want in order for her to go back to sleep. She lifted her butt up a little to help him get her panties off smoothly.

"Damn baby, you're already wet for me," he cooed. Jonte loved everything about Farren, she was so sweet to him.

He entered her with ease and started stroking her real slow, her pussy started singing back to him. "Yes baby," she encouraged him to do it just like that.

Farren and Jonte's sex was different for the both of them because Jonte wasn't into making love or taking his time with any female. With Farren, he knew he had to treat her with nothing but the utmost respect. Jonte learned how to bring Farren to a climax in other ways without using his dick. Jonte pulled out of her pussy without warning and started licking and sucking on her pussy.

She rubbed her hands through his tiny curls that lay atop his head, Jonte knew his tongue was lethal, it was long and fat. He took his time snaking it in and out of her pussy. She knew she was cumming, but she didn't want him to stop, so she squeezed her eyes shut and tried to refrain from screaming, "I'm fucking cumming all in your mouth," from the top of her lungs.

Jonte knew Farren had about two orgasms by now. She was so selfish in bed sometimes, instead of her flipping him over and riding his dick so he can nut and they both can get some much needed sleep. She was trying to fuck all the life out of him until she was done.

Jonte's legs started giving out when he tried to fuck Farren from the side, he flopped down and held his leg.

"You tired?" she asked, panting.

"Man get your lazy ass up here and ride my dick," he commanded.

Farren bit her lip, she loved when Jonte got ghetto with her, that shit did something to her. She threw her hair over her shoulder and climbed on top of daddy and started taking him on a very wild ride.

Jonte slapped her ass, encouraging her to keep it up and ride his dick real fast just the way she was doing. Farren was moaning so loud, her perky titties were flopping all over the place. Jonte stuck his finger in her mouth in an attempt to muffle her moans.

She was going crazy on his dick and couldn't contain her emotions.

Finally.

They came. They came together and it felt so good. It took Farren forever to get her breathing back to normal.

Jonte wiped her body down and brought her body closer to his and rubbed her back.

"You just made my night so much better," he told her.

"Why you say that bae?" she asked, playing with the hair on his stomach. This nigga was so sexy.

"I don't know, something just not right. You know how you gotta trust your gut?" he said.

Farren knew what he meant but what she wanted to know was what he was referring too.

"Yeah, but what's wrong?" she asked.

"It's like I don't think it will be a fuck nigga that will be my downfall, I think it's going to end up being the ones closest to me," he yawned and closed his eyes. Today had been entirely too long and he just wanted to go to sleep, especially after that quick love session.

Farren didn't know what to say that so she said nothing, all she could do was pray that God revealed his enemies to Jonte.

"Mommy come on," Noel pulled her mother's arm.

She looked up at Jonte. "I love you," she told him.

"I know, be careful," he told her, eyeing her wondering what was on her mind.

Farren knew how to get in touch with him, if she needed to. He wasn't worried that she was able to handle herself, Farren was a thorough woman and she was a rare breed and truly in a league of her own.

Farren spirits were down after visiting her baby daddy Jonte, she knew that these visits were going to always be the same way, so no point in crying over spilled milk.

She was grateful that Morgan was smiling and playing again, it had been so long since she seen her fat mama laughing. Seeing her daddy had Morgan feeling too good.

Farren parked her truck in one of the parking spots in the front of the nursing home, she helped Morgan and Noel down from their seats and they went to sign in at the front desk to visit her mother-in-law. Farren told Mike to remind her to stop by the financial office so she could pay Mrs. Knight's stay up for another year, she knew that would make Christian happy

Noel covered her nose up. "It stinks in here," she whispered to her big brother.

"Mrs. Knight? It's me, Farren," she said once they found her room.

Mrs. Knight was laying in her hospital bed with her body turned towards to the window.

Farren went over to her side and took Michael with her, "Mrs. Knight, do you remember me?" she asked.

She just stared at her.

Farren moved a little over to the right so that she could see Michael.

Mrs. Knight rose up and smiled, she reached her hand out to Michael and he jumped.

"That's your grandmother, stop it," she fussed.

"Chrissy," Mrs. Knight said proudly.

Farren had tears in her eyes from what Christian told her, his mom hadn't spoken in years.

"Chrissy, where is your daddy?" she asked. Michael got closer to his grandma, and she rubbed her hands on his face.

Morgan whispered into Noel's ear, "Who is Chrissy?" she asked.

"My daddy, girl," she told her.

Mrs. Knight spent the next hour fussing about Chloe and Courtney being bad while Christian was away at school.

The nurses couldn't believe that she finally opened her mouth, the Doctor came in and told Farren that familiar faces were good for people who suffered with dementia and Alzheimer's.

They said their goodbyes and left.

"She was so pretty," Noel said.

"Why you acting like you don't know grandma?" Michael asked.

"Shut up cus you didn't remember her either." Noel hit him in the back of his head.

"Both of y'all be quiet. Okay, two more stops and then we're getting on the road."

"The road? We not flying" Michael asked.

"Nope, good old fashioned road trip with mommy and Beyoncé," she said laughing.

"Beyoncé? Man put me on a plane. I'm old enough," Michael said, he was mad.

"No you are not," Noel said. She swore she was somebody's mama.

Farren turned the radio up and headed to the gravesite. She had grabbed tons of roses and sunflowers at the nursing home where her mother in law resided. Her mom had spent the night with them last night, so she had said her goodbyes to her mother already.

"I don't wanna get out," Noel said.

"Me neither," Mike said.

"Y'all don't want to say goodbye to your daddy or your sister?" Farren asked, her feelings hurt.

"Nah ma, I'm good," Mike said.

Their mom didn't understand that was something they weren't ready to do.

Farren got out the car and slammed the door, she stopped by Carren's grave first. "Hey baby, I miss you so much," she said, laying the roses down.

"I love you and Noel reminds me so much of you. Girl, it's crazy," Farren said.

She held back a few tears. "I hope you're not up there giving your daddy no attitude, you're still a little girl to us," she said.

Wiping her face, Farren touched the grave for a few seconds wishing that it was her daughter for just one more time. Farren just wanted to hug her and love her a little longer. Carren left way before it was her time, she wanted to travel the world playing soccer, and she wanted to go to Spellman College like her big cousin Kennedy. Some shit just wasn't fair to her, she couldn't believe she had buried her daughter. Anger swept over, she fucking hated Bianchi and everything that came from him.

Farren didn't have to walk far to Christian's grave, he was buried right next to his daughter, father and sister.

"Hi you," she said with a warm smile.

It was as if Christian said hey back, she felt a warm sensation come over her.

"I'm moving to Atlanta, Georgia," she told him.

"It's nothing else here for me, Jonte done went and got his ass locked up," she told Christian.

"Well, it's a lil chilly out here and the kids are being spoiled brats as usual," she told her husband.

Farren missed Christian Knight, she missed him in secret, and she probably would never tell anyone that. See, some people didn't understand love. But guess what? Love wasn't for people to understand, love was between two people and in some cases three people. Love wasn't about other people's opinions, it didn't care what this person or that person thought. Love couldn't be stopped because your home girl felt like he wasn't the one, love overcame all bullshit. Do not get it twisted, now sometimes love hurts but it shouldn't hurt twice.

Farren wondered if Christian Knight ever really loved her, did he ever really care as much as he put on to. Farren needed confirmation, a sign or a wonder, but she knew that she really needed to just let it go and move on.

In her downtime, she caught herself reading old, old, old text messages and busting out laughing. That damn Christian Knight was so arrogant, but it was the one thing that she loved about him.

His demeanor, his fly, his ambition, his desire to see her become all she could be.

Farren remembered one day she was at home…

"Babe!" Christian Knight called out.

She was very surprised to hear his voice. "Chrissy? What are you doing home so early," she asked.

She looked a mess, her hair was dirty and it was braided sloppily. She had on a big t-shirt and some white granny panties, Farren had spent the day cleaning up and getting their house together. She had just officially moved in with him in his nice home, but it wasn't her. Farren felt like Christian's ex-fiancée had probably helped him design a few of the rooms and it bothered her. The day before, she spent a lot of time at Pier One Imports, buying all new kitchenware, Farren didn't plan on cooking in anything after that bitch. The way Christian had described his ex, made her feel like she was a little psychotic. The first night after she moved in, once Christian had left to run his normal morning errands, she burned sage and prayed all those past demons up and out of that house. There was no way in hell, she was going to be spending the majority of her time with him and feeling some type of way about his ex, Miranda. Although, Christian didn't believe in discussing the past with the present she had got all the dirt she needed from him messy ass sisters. Farren made a mental note to keep Chloe, Christian's sister, at bay. She was too friendly too fast and Farren wasn't feeling that all.

"I got you some books," he told her, dropping a bag that read Barnes and Nobles on the front.

"Books?" she was confused.

"Yeah, a few books that I want you to read, so we can discuss them together over dinner," he told her, kissing her mouth.

"I need to bathe." Farren tried to move around him and take off her rubber gloves.

"I'm not stunting that shit. Why are you cleaning? I have a housekeeper," he told her, taking the sponge out of her hand.

"I fired her," she said.

"Why? I love her, she's been cleaning my house for years," Christian asked in frustration.

"I'm capable of cooking and cleaning for you," she told him, voice dripped with attitude and hands on her hip. Every now and then Farren brought out that Hardy girl act to remind Christian Knight's ass that she wasn't the one to play with.

No bitch would be cleaning her house as long as she had two arms and two legs that worked just fine.

Christian smiled, bent down and bit her cheek, she was so sexy to him.

"I want you to read those books, we are going to work on elevating your thinking and your conversation. I plan on introducing you to all of my legal buddies. Mark my words, when you finish law school you're going to climb to the top of the ladder," he said with so much confidence.

Farren loved that he was just as excited about her career as she was, it made her feel so special that he took time out of his very busy day to buy her books for her to read. Christian Knight was always sending her links to articles and stuff for her to check out.

If Christian Knight didn't teach her anything else about life, not even love, it was that one needed to work on becoming the best person that you could be. He taught her to be receptive to everything, never think you're too good to learn something new. Christian treated everybody with respect and Farren admired that about him.

"I love you Chrissy." Farren blew a kiss towards his grave and walked off.

Noel complained once she returned to the car, "You were out there forever, we're hungry."

Farren wanted to slap her, but they were young and didn't understand the importance of life yet, so she ignored her and headed to her last stop per Jonte's request: Mari's house.

Farren entered the code in the gate, after putting it in for so long she knew it without even having to look.

"I miss auntie," Morgan said.

"I bet you do, she used to let y'all run over the house," Farren said, shaking her head.

The "For Sale" sign is what took her by surprise. When did Mari leave? And why did she leave without telling her brother-in-law? Farren wasn't stunting her ass, but Jonte was worried sick about the well-being of his nieces and nephews.

Farren peeped through the window near the garage, and all of the cars were gone. The garage was completely cleaned out. She wondered what money did she have to move and where would she go.

Farren had too much on her plate to worry about another grown woman, she would just pass her discovery on to Jonte and let him handle the rest.

Chapter Ten

"Noel, when was the last time you had a beating?" Farren asked her daughter. She had been on ten all day and now that the sun had fell she was even more turnt. Farren regretted the day when she said she would be a stay-at-home mom, her kids were bad, real bad. As soon as school started back, she told herself she was going to get her a damn job. So far, Atlanta had been treating them lovely, Farren took the children to all of the museums Georgia had to offer, and she really wanted her kids to appreciate everything they had. She made a chore chart for them to follow and they had been doing well so far.

Farren had begun going to church and everything. She and Kool had been kicking it tough whenever he was in town. The Cartel had increased his drops, so he was always gone trying to make a dollar. She knew that she needed to be done with street niggas, but it was something about Kool that really attracted him to her. The time they spent together was always memorable, and she was really feeling him so far.

They hadn't argued or anything, Kool wasn't with none of that anyway. He treated Farren with the most respect and every time they spent time together, she was putting him on to something new. Even when he was away, she was on his mind.

"I'm not even doing nothing," Noel said.

"I'm folding clothes and you just bouncing all around the damn house. Do you want to help mommy fold clothes?" she asked, sarcastically.

"No ma'am, I'm going to just go to my room," she told her mom and ran off.

Farren pressed play on the television and resumed her show, she loved the talk show *The Real*, and she recorded every show and watched it at night.

Her phone ringing caused her to have to smack her lips again, if it wasn't her mom or her sister or Kool she wasn't answering. She had just smoked her a blunt, and was sipping on some coconut Cîroc watching her girl Tamar, she didn't want to be bothered and damn sure wasn't in the mood to be on the phone either.

But the "305" area code caused her to second guess her decision.

Mario's number was saved, it couldn't be anybody else…Mr. Bianchi.

Farren raked her brain trying to figure out what the fuck could he want, the ringing stopped before she could come to a conclusion.

But, oh better believe it started ringing again.

She answered, knowing damn well if she didn't he would have somebody at her door.

"He…hello," her voice was a lil shaky.

"Farren Knight, how are you?" Mr. Bianchi asked, cheerfully.

"Well," she said, Farren wasn't giving him nothing more nothing less.

"I heard that your house in Smyrna is in a really good neighborhood, the school districts out there are superb as well," he told her.

Farren rolled her eyes. That was this slimy motherfucker way of letting her know that no matter where she moved to, he would always know. But the thing was, Farren wasn't hiding or running from him, she was minding her business and attempting to leave all the bullshit in the past and raise her children and stack her money.

"To what do I owe the pleasure of this call?" she asked.

"I need you in Miami tomorrow at seven p.m. sharp. You remember how to get my house, don't you?" he asked.

"Tomorrow?" Farren asked, to be sure that she heard him correctly.

"That's what I said, isn't it?" he said, sarcastically.

"Why?" she asked out of curiosity.

"I'll answer all questions tomorrow," he told her and hung the phone up.

Farren couldn't believe this shit. Why did she even answer the phone? She knew that he wasn't calling to say hello, and asking how she was doing. The Cartel didn't make social calls at all.

Farren hoped that Kennedy wasn't sleep yet. She needed to drop the kids off tonight, so tomorrow she wouldn't be rushing to the airport.

Thank God she was up and bored, her husband worked at night so the kids coming over would be the highlight of her day.

Farren rushed and threw them a few clothes in one big bag. She normally wasn't so unorganized, but she needed to get back home and prepare her mind to be in the presence of the man who probably ordered the hit on Christian Knight even if he didn't, his son still killed her oldest daughter, Carren. Farren just hated everything about the Bianchi family.

"When are you coming back?" Noel asked, sadly.

"If not tomorrow then the day after, I promise."

"Baby, I'm going to tell Jonte to call your cell phone so please keep the phone charged" she kissed all of her children and told Kennedy thank you for the millionth time.

Farren called Kool once she got back home. She didn't like being home by herself at night, and she always felt like something bad was going to happen.

"Bae," he said, once he finally answered the phone.

"I gotta go to Miami in the morning," she told him.

"Damn, that's crazy cus I do too, I just got the call" he said.

Farren was now wanting to know what the hell this meeting was about tomorrow.

"I miss you," she told him.

"Miss you too boo. What are you doing? You packed?" he asked.

"No, I'll probably shop when I get there. I hate carrying a suitcase through the airport," she told him.

"Hollywood," he said laughing.

"Where are you?" Farren questioned.

"Hotel in Baltimore," he told her.

"You got your ticket yet?" she asked.

"Nah, they got a jet and all that," he said. Kool really didn't like talking on the phone and he wish Farren would change the subject or hang up.

"Aww okay."

"Say boo, hit my line when you land tomorrow," he told her.

"Okay, I will," she told him.

Farren wasn't taking a shower tonight, she kept having this weird vision that someone was going to pull her out the shower and stab her ass to death. Farren got cozy on the couch, with two guns and a knife. She didn't even turn the television up loud. She wanted to hear everything, from a car coming up the street. Farren even stopped the dryer because it was too loud. She was a woman that trusted her gut always, because it had never steered her wrong.

The next morning came rather quickly. Farren stood and stretched, her couch wasn't the comfiest.

She made her a cup of coffee, ate a bagel with cream cheese and tossed a few strawberries and grapes back.

Farren took a quick shower and unwrapped her hair.

She wasn't planning on taking anything on the plane, but her Oprah magazine and she opened her safe to put her little black book in her purse.

Thank God that her flight departed on time. She arrived in Ft. Lauderdale, Florida in good timing and caught a cab to Miami, Florida and went straight to the mall. It had been so long since Farren went shopping and she tore the mall down. Farren used to have a crazy shoe fetish, but with this year's back to back events she hadn't really spent any money on herself. She caught an Uber to the W Hotel, checked in her hotel and finally caught up on the sleep that she didn't get last night.

Farren knew not to expect to hear from Kool until after the meeting. He hated these Roundtable meetings. Kool preferred to handle his business from afar.

She hummed some old Mary J. Blige, as she slid on her stockings and dressed herself in a fitted black dress by Burberry, the front had three plaid buttons in the chest area.

Farren had more black pumps in her shoe collection than the average woman, she removed the top to a brand new pair of Prada black pumps. Farren put on some red lipstick and sprayed perfume behind her ears and on her wrist. She was pleased with her appearance, as she already assumed a tinted black Escalade truck was waiting on her in the lobby. How this man always knew her whereabouts creeped her out.

Farren tapped her manicured fingers on the door handle, taking in the outside air and everything that was in sight. Miami was so beautiful, but it was too fast-paced for her. Farren was old, although she didn't look like she was, she was old.

The driver opened her door and helped her down. She smiled at the cute young Mexican boy and told him, "Thank you."

And in return he said, "De nada senorita."

Farren liked them young, it made her feel like a sexy MILF and a cougar. She knew she still had it going on though, her groove had never left.

The first person that Farren saw was Mario, but he didn't speak so she didn't either. She arrived to the Bianchi estate an hour before the meeting.

The housekeeper came around and asked a few members of The Cartel if they wanted a drink or something to eat, a few accepted and the newcomers included Farren declined.

Kool entered, he nodded to Farren and she didn't respond to his facial gesture. She would have her lips all over him later on tonight, so there were no worries.

"Is everyone here?" Farren heard Mr. Bianchi ask.

"Just about, except that nigger Greg," someone from the Caballero family asked.

"Have everyone, come on back," he said.

Farren followed the crowd, it wasn't many of them present.

"Farren, up here," Mr. Bianchi told her, how he even knew she was here.

She shook her head, she was so ready to go.

Mario whispered her ear on the low, "You know he secretly admires your work ethic."

Farren smiled and Kool peeped that shit, but now was not the time. Business first, personal second.

Mr. Bianchi was being incredibly nice to Farren, he pulled her chair out for her and everything, then offered her a cigar which she declined.

"Won't hold y'all long at all," he said, standing up.

"I'm retiring. In exactly one month from today, I will appoint a new head," before he could continue.

Mario yelled out, "Appoint? That's not how this works and you know it."

"Watch your tone," Bianchi warned him.

"Fuck you! I was up next and you know it."

"One day, you're pillow talking saying you want out, but now you want to run it? Make your mind up young boy," he pointed his finger.

Mario looked over at Farren, she was the only person he told that to.

Farren's eyes went back and forth between Bianchi and Mario, she had never repeated anything her and Mario ever discussed with anyone.

"This is bullshit," he said, grabbing his motorcycle helmet and exiting the room.

"As I was saying, because every family has been slacking if you ask me, everyone is up for the seat. That includes Karter, Greg, and Mo," he said.

The families all erupted in argument.

"Get out," he banged on the table and told them.

Everyone got quiet. "Did I stutter? Get the fuck out of my house, see ya next month," he said.

Farren stood, Bianchi grabbed her hand. "Sit," he told her.

She had no choice but to sit, the grip he had on her hand was something serious. Kool looked at her before he left, he would be waiting on her when she got to the hotel. Farren sent him a text, informing him that there was a key at the hotel check-in waiting on him.

"Who would you choose?" he asked.

"I don't know, that's a decision you need to make," she told him.

"Don't sass me. Who do you feel is best, honestly?"

Farren thought long and hard it would be between Greg and Mario, in her personal opinion.

Kool handled his business well, but The Cartel was on some global shit. That took years of wisdom and acquired experience to reach that kind of level.

Farren was so tired once she finally made it back to the hotel, she and Bianchi reviewed notes on literally every single family in The Cartel. She was about to crash as soon as her face hit the pillow.

Kool was sitting on the couch, on his iPad looking at some watches. He felt that he deserved some new pieces, he had been working tirelessly days in and nights out.

"Hi babe," Farren said once she entered the hotel room.

"Damn, you look tired. Come here," he called out, once he saw she was bypassing him.

"Kool, I'm tired. Come in here," she told him.

Farren was trying to take a quick shower so she can go to sleep.

He put the iPad down and went into their bedroom, "What's going on?" he asked

She undressed quietly, she had a lot on her mind but she didn't want to think or talk about it right now, she just wanted to rest.

"He's trying to do things fairly, I will say that," she told him.

"Well when we walked out, a few of them folks was tripping about how he's going about it," Kool told her.

"I don't think he fucked with Mario's daddy, that's what I think the issue is" she said and got in the shower.

"So what did he meet with you about?" he asked.

"We went through some files," her answers was real short. Farren didn't want to mix business with personal, because at the end of the day her meetings with Bianchi were confidential and none of Kool's business.

"Who are you going to vote for?" he asked.

"Who said I had a vote?" she shot back.

"Don't try and play me like a lame," he said.

"Play you like a lame?" she asked. Farren got out the shower so fast.

"You talking to me?" she asked, butt-naked she stood before Kool.

Farren wasn't with the shit, if he wanted to ask her something, as a man he needed to just come out and say it.

"Who are you voting for? I'm asking one simple question" he told her.

"I don't know yet," and that was the honest truth.

"Fa sho," Kool said and walked out of the bathroom, slamming the door behind him. It was obvious the nigga was in her feelings, but Farren was too tired to kiss his ass, so she dried off and got in bed naked.

Kool smoked his life away that night, he knew that Bianchi probably felt like he was at the bottom of the totem pole. It was no secret that the man liked Greg more, but Kool knew he had been doing a good job and deserved a fair chance just as everyone else.

He just had to work harder in the next three weeks and do all he could to show that he was capable of leading The Cartel. Kool tried to find his way to the bathroom which was located in the bedroom, Farren had the curtains closed and the room was pitch fucking dark, plus he was super high.

He stumbled over her suitcase, knocking her purse over which was on top of the suitcase. He bent down to put the contents that fell out back in the purse until he came across "the little black book". His mind went back to the first time he ever laid eyes on

Farren, in their meeting at the bookstore when he was being vetted by The Cartel. She was writing notes on him in her "little black book".

Kool looked at the bed and Farren was knocked out, he knew she was because of how tired she appeared. He grabbed the notebook, closed the bedroom door and went to sit back in the small sitting area that came with their suite.

Kool scanned the notebook, then started from the beginning, reading detailed notes about each of the families. He didn't know that Farren was involved heavily in the day to day decisions they made from produce, extortion, slavery, prostitution. She even advised on locations to where they did drop-offs.

She had estimated numbers of how much each family made monthly and everything.

The information in here was fucking crazy, it was like a Cartel bible. Kool spent hours reading all of the information.

"What the fuck are you doing?" Farren asked, with a gun in her hand.

"Whoa, put that gun down," he told her.

"Why do you have my notebook?" she ignored his question.

Farren got up to pee and grab her phone out of her purse to text Mario, she wasn't able to sleep comfortably without knowing that they were still cool. She wanted to explain her side of the story and tell him that she would never discuss Mr. Bianchi with him.

"No reason. I was just looking through it, no big deal baby," he said.

"No big deal Kool, come on now. Really?" she asked.

Farren was not with the shit and she didn't appreciate him snooping through her things, especially something like that. There was enough information in that notebook for him to bring The Cartel down or takeover. She couldn't allow him to do either because she damn sure wasn't going down with their ass. Farren had been telling herself she needed to burn the fucking notebook anyway.

"Farren put the gun down," he yelled.

"Shut up! Did you even like me? I'm just asking because why do you have that. I don't understand," she asked, using the gun to push her hair out of her face. Kool eyes got big, it was like his sweet Farren disappeared and some new evil bitch appeared.

"Yes, I like you. Hell, I feel like I'm falling in love with you," he told her.

Farren laughed, no actually she snorted. She found him so funny tonight.

Farren remembered a conversation she had with Christian Knight at Ruth's Chris the day before he was killed in his home.

"Say Farren, let me tell you something about them Cartel niggas, they're all snakes. All of them. Do you hear me? They will kill their brother to impress Bianchi's old ass," he said.

"But why?" she asked.

Christian chuckled. "At the end of the day, people especially hood niggas, all dream about making it into The Cartel. Keep your head up and if you can't get out, don't make any friends. None," he told her.

"I don't," she told him.

"But you will, some of them gone try to get you, just off the strength that you was my woman and they know that I was the main nigga running shit in there," he said cockily.

Farren rolled her eyes, it wasn't every day that you met with niggas like Christian Knight.

Farren snapped back into reality. "Where did you get that gun from?" she asked him.

"I got here on a private jet. How did you get a gun, you don't trust me?" he asked.

"No, it's not me that don't trust you, it's Bianchi. He gave me this gun before I left his house," she said and shot him in the arm.

Kool saw the blood and his adrenaline started rushing. He wanted to kill her, but he actually liked her and right now was just a big misunderstanding. However, to Farren it didn't look that way and the mindset she had right now, can't nobody be trusted not even the man you was sucking and fucking. Farren continued, "I sat in his house all night, convincing him that you worked hard and with a little more training you would be awesome. However, I wake up to pee and I see you going through my shit. Oh hell nah," she said, shooting him in his leg.

She was now pissed.

"I don't know if you forgot who the fuck I am, but I'm the original Connect's Wife," she told him and shot him in his chest. She shot away from his heart because she wasn't done talking.

Farren paced the room. "Why do people like trying me? What y'all think cus I like to cook dinner and pick flowers in my garden, I won't shoot? I'm filled with anger, you knew not to fuck with me."

Kool was groaning in pain, "Listen to me..." he pleaded.

Farren bit her lip. "No, I'm done talking," she told him and shot him in his chest, but this time she hit her target perfectly.

She called Bianchi back to back a few times before he answered. It was late, she figured he was sleeping. She wasn't planning on killing her supposed to be boyfriend tonight, all Farren got up to do was pee. "I need you to send someone to my room," she said and hung up the phone. Farren went to the living room table, and picked up his blunt, grabbed her little black book from off the floor, then went and sat on the bed. What Farren didn't realize what that this was really only the beginning…the fuckery had just started.

Chapter Eleven

Farren didn't feel any emotion behind killing Kool and that scared her, she had never been one of those heartless people. Farren loved life, she thanked God every single morning when she woke up for giving her another day to wake up and do things differently. Farren was grateful that she and Kool didn't get too attached, his death didn't bother her. In fact, she left before the clean-up crew even got there and headed back to Atlanta. Mr. Bianchi warned her to keep her eyes open and if she felt like she wanted protection to just let him know. She didn't know why he suggested that, she wasn't worried about anyone knowing Kool coming to haunt her down, she had only been around his crew one time. Farren didn't go out in Atlanta, in fact she couldn't recall the last time she had went somewhere.

"Did y'all have fun with Auntie Kennedy?" she asked her children on the way back home.

"Yeah I guess, she talk too much," Noel said.

Farren couldn't do anything but shake her head, her daughter was too grown.

"She wakes up happy and goes to bed happy," Mike said.

"What's wrong with that? I'm the same way," she told them.

"No you're not mommy," Noel told her mom.

Before she could respond, someone hit her from the side and caused her to swerve across the highway.

"What the fuck?" Farren yelled.

She didn't even see that car coming alongside her, Farren got control of the car. One thing Farren could do was drive. She had been driving other folk's car since she was ten years old.

Farren looked in her rearview mirror and didn't see the car that hit her at all. She was going to chalk that up as being a simple mistake, but if that shit happened again, kids in the car and all she was pulling her gun out and shooting the fucking highway up. A person could come for her all day but do not bring harm to her children, she had already lost one daughter and didn't plan on losing another. For her kids, Farren would lay her life down on the line, they had nobody but her. Their daddy was gone and the other was in jail only a few months in on a forty-year sentence.

Thank God, they made it home safely and when they pulled up there was a 2015 Bentley Coupe sitting in her driveway.

"Ma, you got me a car?" Mike asked.

"Uh you can barely drive," she told him, getting out of the car and slipping her gun in her waist, discreetly, so the kids wouldn't see. However, she had the nosiest kids in the world.

"Get back in the car," she yelled to them.

"Why it's hot?" Noel complained.

"Wait a minute," she told them.

Farren walked to the car and looked around it, she got on her stomach and looked under the car for a device or some type of bomb or something. The next Roundtable meeting was coming up and Farren knew that people thought she had the final say-so, but she really didn't see why her vote was so important. Farren failed to realize just how important her dad's position was in The Cartel, she really didn't understand.

Farren opened the car and felt under all of the seats, she opened all of the compartments and consoles looking for anything, but what she did find when she pulled the visor over the passenger door was a handwritten note, "Enjoy from the O'Meyer family!"

"What the fuck!" Farren said in surprise, Farren was going to park the car in her driveway. It was too nice for her not to want to drive, but she would wait in case she was being watched by other families. She didn't want to give anyone the impression that she was voting the O'Meyer family, although they had always been very nice to her when she came to visit them for their monthly meetings. Farren didn't like how they handled business, so for that reason she wouldn't be voting for them.

Farren helped her kids in the house and she could have sworn that she turned her oven off before she left. She had made the kids some lasagna, but she turned the oven off before she left, she was sure of it.

"Y'all wait right here," she told them, pulling her gun out and walking in the kitchen.

"Mama got a gun," Noel said, covering her eyes.

She ignored her daughter and walked in each room making sure nothing else was out of place. She didn't want to be ran out of her own home.

Farren told the kids to go to their rooms and she would call them when dinner was ready.

Farren called Mario. "Hi," she said once he answered.

"Sup," he said, dryly.

"Have I ever gave a reason for you to not trust me?" she asked.

"Nah, but I confided in you and you only," he said.

"And you still can," she told him.

"It's no friends in this business baby girl. Tell your baby daddy I said what up though," he said and hung the phone up.

Farren's heart beat, dropped she prayed like hell Mario wouldn't be petty and fuck with Jonte. He had nothing to do with this and she didn't talk to Mr. Bianchi about him. She promised to God she didn't.

Farren wasn't feeling this, she had a bad feeling that things were only about to get worse. She laid down on the couch with her eyes closed praying that this Roundtable meeting hurried up and came, she was thinking about moving to St. Thomas to get away from the bullshit. Farren really didn't understand that The Cartel was like the plague, no matter where you think you could go to sleep in peace and enjoy life, they was coming for your ass. St. Thomas, Cancun, Ethiopia, Madrid, Kuwait to Iraq it didn't matter, they would find you and if needed be kill you. She signed her life over when she went to that first meeting with the Sanchez family. That's why Christian Knight told Farren if her daddy really loved her, he would have never asked his daughter to "help him out". Christian Knight wasn't sure of his assumptions, but if he remembered correctly Farad, Farren's father, had done some real shiesty shit. He either slept with one of The Cartel's wives and had a daughter or something trifling. He tried to pay his way out of his mess, but he only dug a deeper hole. The girl who was allegedly his daughter was being raised by her grandmother because the mom had been killed and as Farad is known to do, he never stepped up to the plate and acknowledged his daughter.

Either way it went, Farad was secretly a snake. He would sell his votes all the time, which is why the families assumed they could do the same thing to Farren. But she was unaware of all of this, Farren was a really fair person, practicing law for over twenty years gave her the experience to be able to discern and make the best decision for the party she was representing. Although, Bianchi didn't fuck with Farren's dad or her husband, he did love Dice a lot and he knew that Farren was different from her dad. Farren was a woman who handled her business well, he would never tell her that she had helped make him a lot of money this year, by weeding out the bad. Farren had become his voice of reason. The night of the meeting when they left, he apologized for the death of her daughter and told her that he missed his son every single day.

Don't get it twisted Farren still didn't fuck with him, but she respected him for apologizing. Farren asked him if he killed Christian Knight and he told her no. She didn't know if he was telling the truth or not, so for that reason her guards were up and she ain't trust nobody; not even Kool's ass and apparently Mario either.

Farren enjoyed her night with her kids, her kids were her reason for breathing. The next morning they were up bright and early to do some school shopping.

"Ma, Uncle Greg is here," Noel came running in her mother's room, smiling.

"What?" she knew her ears were playing trick on her. Farren did smoke this morning as she sat on the toilet, the lasagna didn't agree with her stomach because she rarely ate beef and that was all she had in the freezer at the time.

"Uncle Greg and he bought me a *Frozen* book bag," she said.

"Go in your room and lock the door," she told her.

Farren got her gun and walked into the foyer of her home. Her heart was beating fast and her hand wouldn't stop shaking. It was something about Greg that irritated her, Farren's jaw was tight and her eye was twitching. In his presence, she was immediately irritated filled with anger.

"Damn sis, that's how we do it now?" Greg said, looking as if his feelings was hurt, but she knew he was just fucking with her.

"I've been on a roll lately, so wasup?" she asked, walking into the kitchen and leaning on the counter that was right behind the knives. Farren had no problem stabbing or shooting this nigga, she had learned how to do it all.

"Just coming to check on my god kids," he told her, grabbing a banana out of the fruit basket on the kitchen table.

"We didn't see you at Chrissy's funeral? I'm sure you got the memo that someone shot him?" Farren asked, with a smirk on her face.

She wanted this pussy nigga to lie and tell her some bullshit. "Yeah me and my bitch was out of town, didn't see no point in rushing back home for an hour long funeral," he said, shrugging his shoulders.

Farren couldn't believe the nerve of this nigga. "How can I help you, Greg?" she questioned.

"Well, since you wanna be rude there's no point in me beating around the bush. I'm not buying you any cars, nor burning your house down to get your attention. I just came to tell you that if you don't vote for me, I'ma kill your kids while you watch, then I'm going to kill your ass. Okay?" he said with a smile.

Farren's heart stopped, she could not believe this nigga had the nerve to say that and then smile after.

"Get out of my house!" she yelled.

"I'm leaving anyway, kiss my godchildren for me," he told her. He took the banana out of the peel and left the peel on the table.

"Don't be caught slipping on a banana peel," he said, winked his eye at her and left out of the same door as he came in.

Farren waited until she heard his car pull off, she fell down to her knees and tried to catch her breath. She couldn't breathe. What in the fuck did she get herself into? A nigga that she knew for a fact broke bread with her husband just threatened to kill her and her children with no remorse. Farren knew that he was the one that killed Christian Knight, it was definitely confirmed now.

Farren called Bianchi and he didn't answer the phone. She wondered what the fuck was his protection going to do to give her a peace of mind, she was fucking paranoid. Farren didn't want to be in that house anymore, she wanted to leave now.

The only place she knew that nothing would happen to her and if it did it was some niggas ready to kill on sight for her was her hood.

Farren gathered her kids and told them to come on, she had never driven so fast to get to her next destination, which was the AIRPORT.

Farren and the kids went straight to the condo once they landed, she watched her kid sleep in the only bed in the condo. Farren paced the floor the majority of the night, with her little black book in her hand. She didn't like being uncomfortable or not able to do what she wanted.

A few days later after leaving both of her phones off, the children weren't feeling being cooped up in the tiny condo and Morgan had started crying for her daddy. Damn, Farren felt horrible for leaving her phones off after the threat that Mario dropped on her before hanging up in her face.

Farren asked her son Michael, "Did Jonte call your phone?"

"It's been dead," he told her, and went back to playing the game.

"What teenager lets their phone go dead?" Farren asked, her son was only concerned with *Sportscenter* and playing his videogames. Noel had his cell phone more than he did, playing games and taking selfies. She really loved herself and Farren was grateful that she was confident there was a time where you couldn't get Noel to smile because she didn't like how crooked her teeth were.

"Can we go to the nail shop and get some steak? I'm bored," Noel complained.

Farren wanted to tell her hell no, but she knew that she couldn't keep her own kids hostage. The entire family showered one by one and got dressed to spend a day in the city.

The day was actually what Farren needed, she laughed and had fun with her kids. They all had awesome personalities. They ended their night at Ruth's Chris, her kids wasn't chicken tenders kids; they liked salmon, lobster, calamari and steak!

"Ma'am, your tab has already been taken care of," the waitress told her when Farren asked for the check.

"By who?" Farren asked.

"Those people behind you," she pointed, Farren and her kids turned around to see Jose Vergas and his family eating food. Jose caught Farren's stare and raised his hand up. Now what in the hell was Jose doing in New York when his ass knew good and well he lived in Colombia?

Shit was getting out of hand, Farren knew she wasn't going back to the condo tonight. She and the kids went to Hardy projects.

Farren made the kids go in the house while she went back into The Courtyard to talk to Spider, Jonte's right hand.

"You heard from your boy?" she asked.

"Nah, not this week, you?" he questioned.

"No and that's not normal. He normally calls me at least twice a day," she said.

"I'm sure everything is good. That nigga probably in the hole or something," he told her.

"Didn't you get released when Mari did?" Farren asked, it was weird to her that Mari hadn't called or asked for money.

"Yeah, but you know I don't really fuck with that broad, some nigga picked her up. They kept us separate the whole time though," he told her.

"What nigga?" Farren needed to know, Mari had been talking about some imaginary boyfriend for years, but no one had ever seen him. Farren thought she was always lying, but never said anything to her about it, not wanting to hurt her feelings.

Mari wanted love after Johan but what woman wouldn't.

Farren wasn't thinking about love right now, hell at this point all she cared about was staying alive and making it to see next year. Her gut was telling her to never ever let her guard down, she wasn't going anywhere without her gun and a knife In Hardy, she was good. This was her hood, and they wasn't letting anybody that looked unfamiliar walk through here, Cartel or not.

The next day, Farren sent the local knuckleheads to the store to get tons of meat so they could have a BBQ, she wanted a grilled turkey burger with onions and cheese. Her mom was in the kitchen making some baked beans and potato salad, Noel and Morgan was trying to help but they was really getting on their grandmother's nerves, but she was trying to not to show it. Farren's mom did not like kids, she cursed too much and her patience was thin, truth be told her kids raised themselves because their mama was always at work and when she wasn't at work she was in the streets. Farren had been washing clothes and taking care of herself since she was in the third grade, her mama taught her how to pay bills and all of that when she was in middle school. You know how most parents, helped you study for exams and assist you with research for scholarships and applying to colleges. Whelp, Farren handled all of her own school business, she applied to schools on her own and when she got accepted she didn't hear her mother to tell her congrats. Her mother used to tell her all of the time, work hard for you, if you wait on an applause from me or from anybody. You'll be disappointed every single time baby girl. Farren kept that mindset her whole life, so as she matriculated through high school, and trail blazed through college despite her mitigating circumstances she patted herself on the back every single time. Farren rewarded herself because she was proud of the woman she was becoming. Educated and proud that she didn't have to fuck or suck anyone to get to where she was. Farren's mother was very proud of her, she just wasn't a woman of many words, she spoke when it was necessary. Farren wanted better for herself, her mother didn't need the diamonds or designer clothes, and she enjoyed her three bedroom apartment that the government paid the majority of the rent.

Farren heard someone calling her name from outside, Mrs. Nakia kept her balcony door open, she had to hear everything going in The Courtyard, and she never wanted to miss nothing.

Farren peeped out the curtain. "What?" she asked.

"Some girl is out here looking for you, named Kim?" one of the local crackheads, Junebug, told her.

"Kim?" she asked again to be sure.

"Yeah lil thick bitch," he motioned with his hands a woman's silhouette.

Farren pulled the balcony door closed, "Why you close my door?" her mother asked.

"Shh…I'm trying to think," she told her mom.

"What's wrong?" she asked, still hooking her baked beans up. She loved when there was a BBQ in the Courtyard, cooking was her favorite pastimes along with drinking beer and playing cards.

After Farren told her who was in the Courtyard to visit her, her mama asked, "And you in here hiding like a lil bitch for what?"

"Ma, why you had to even say that? Who's hiding? I'm just not with the popping up," she said and stood. Farren put her gun in the back of her jeans, pulled her t-shirt down and left the apartment.

Farren walked through the Courtyard and to the parking lot, Kim was leaning on her Porsche.

"Damn girl, I gotta come to your hood to get in touch with you?" she joked.

Farren wasn't laughing. "Wasup?" she asked.

"Just checking on you. You haven't been answering the phone," Kim said.

She looked sincere, but Farren knew that she was about her money so if she came to place her bid then hey, she really wasted her time coming out here.

"I've been okay, better than I expected to feel," Farren said, honestly.

"You heard that dark skinned nigga died right after the meeting? I think Mario shot his ass honestly. He was so mad that night," Kim gossiped. Farren didn't move a muscle as she talked, Farren didn't know what Kim knew.

"Life happens," Farren shrugged.

Kim noticed her stand-off behavior. "You okay friend? You want to go get a drink?" she asked.

"Oh yeah I'm good, just ready to go on vacation," she said, lying.

"No invite?" Kim asked, with a smirk on her face.

Farren saw that the jail was calling her, "I gotta go, thank you for checking up on me," she told Kim and prepared to walk off.

"Farren," she called her name.

Farren turned around, she answered the phone call, "Hi, please give me a second, just one second," she told the caller.

"Yeah?" Farren responded.

"Name your price," she said.

Farren shook her head. She considered Kim a friend, but she knew it was coming, she knew it all along.

"There isn't one Kim," she told her and walked off.

Kim yelled, "Fifty million."

Farren never turned back around, but she did say take care and threw the deuces up.

Damn! Farren had forgotten all about the jail calling and when she called back the woman who answered the phone acted like she didn't know what the fuck Farren was talking about, to say she was frustrated at the current moment was a understatement.

Chapter Twelve

"Are you okay?" Farren asked Jonte for the millionth time. He looked so uncomfortable, she didn't understand why they had to have to be handcuffed to the fucking bed if he was in pain. Three surgeries later to repair his injuries and two and half weeks of coming to visit every day for only an hour was killing Farren more than it was hurting Jonte.

His jaws were broken, so all he could do was nod and shake his head. Farren wanted to fuck Mario up, but Jonte told her that he didn't know who came at him. Nevertheless, Farren knew. She knew for a fact. Farren didn't know who Mr. Bianchi was getting his information from, but it wasn't her. She had never been a woman to pillow talk. Farren's eyes had seen many things and so had her ears and she never said anything, ever.

She personally felt like she and Mario was better than that, but what Farren failed to realize was that Mario felt like he was entitled to the position; especially if Farren's opinion weighed heavily in Mr. Bianchi's eyes. It was the Sanchez family who welcomed her in and didn't disrespect her. It was Mario that pepped her up before she went in meetings with the families. It was Mario that always answered the phone and stopped what he was doing to assist her. It was Mario that had risked his life to come get her from that burning truck when he knew damn well they was trying to kill her ass, or so she thought.

Mario didn't appreciate how this nigga Kool came out of nowhere and swept Farren off of her feet but most importantly, he captured her mind…he wanted Farren.

Mario thought that Greg had killed Kool, in fact everyone thought that he did. It wasn't a secret that Greg killed Christian, at least amongst The Cartel it wasn't. There was speculation that Mr. Bianchi ordered the hit in return for a seat in The Cartel because he knew Christian was trying to come home. Christian's bunk mate was being paid by Mr. Bianchi to report all of Christian's thoughts, movements, he even told Bianchi what that nigga ate for breakfast.

"I hate that this has happened to you, it kills me," she told him, rubbing her hands through his hair and kissing his forehead.

Jonte reached for Farren's phone that was in her other hand. She didn't know what he wanted, but she handed it to him anyway. He typed in her Notes app, "YOU DON'T LOOK THE SAME!"

Farren didn't know how to feel about his comment. Yeah, her eyebrows were a little bushy and she needed to wash her hair, but Jonte was tripping; she was still beautiful. She shook her head at him, rubbed her body and then turned around gripping her fat ass in her camo True Religion jeans.

He motioned for the phone again and she was eager to hand it to him. He typed furiously, "THEY ARE CHANGING YOU!" His eyes were big and they begged for her to run.

Farren's feelings were instantly hurt. "LEAVE," he typed.

Farren told him, "I'm not running from them."

He typed, "I LOVE YOU. I'M GOOD. BYE. TAKE MY KIDS AND GO," he told her.

Farren shook her head. He typed, "YOUR MOM KNOWS MORE THEN SHE'S TELLING YOU, TELL HER YOU WANT TO LEAVE FARREN."

Farren wondered how in the hell did he know what her mom knew, but she wouldn't argue with him. She needed to leave, Bianchi would never leave her alone, even though she gave him that fifty million. The Roundtable meeting was in one week and the amount of gifts she had received were ridiculous. She was receiving anonymous death threats and everything.

Even when she would wake up in the morning, something was always off to her. Farren couldn't lie, she was scared.

She kissed him, wired mouth and all. He couldn't respond back, but she felt the love.

"I love you so much," Farren said with tears in her eyes.

She tried to walk away, but he grabbed her hand. Farren turned around and his eyes told her that he loved her way more than she loved him and Farren knew without a shadow of a doubt that he was the one who never got away, despite the bullshit. Jonte was the Clyde to her Bonnie, the ride to her die, the ever to her forever, he stayed down with her through it all. Loving Farren was not an easy task. She was hard as hell to crack and her guard was up, locked and bolted. Jonte didn't give up on her, he loved her when she didn't feel worthy of love, wiped her tears, and made sweet love to her over and over again.

She held his hand and remembered the first time they said I love you.

"I never wanna leave this place, it's so beautiful," she told him, the condo in which they were staying in Nassau, Bahamas came with a breathtaking view.

"I feel you on that, gotta get back to this money though baby," he told her, kissing her cheek and going back to rolling a blunt. Jonte had linked up with some of the locals at a bar they stopped at on their first day arriving on the island. He had been high as hell their entire vacation and was trying to see how he could take some of it back with him.

"I want you to quit," Farren turned around and told him.

"Farren, we have this talk every other day man, chill. No, I can't do that and I'm not," he snapped.

She wanted to let it go. It was their last day there and she refused to argue with him, but when they got back she wanted peace. She didn't wanna be up all night waiting on him to get there or worrying about whether he would make it out alive when he "handled his business". Farren didn't really understand how Jonte got his money, she honestly thought the nigga did it all, credit card scams, robbed banks, sold drugs, he never lied about being heavily involved in the streets. It was all he knew, he was a hood nigga for real.

"I can take care of us," she told him.

"I'm not going to let you take care of me, I'm not your child." He looked at her and shook his head. Farren was already controlling and bossy, he would be damned if he put his financial stability in her hands.

Farren wanted to tell him that the fast life was never promised to anyone, Farren never worried about Christian Knight because he was the Connect. The Connect didn't risk his life, it was lil nigga like Jonte who did the dirty work. Farren just wanted better for him...for them. She had found love within the crevices of his soul and for her happiness she would do whatever.

"I love you so much," she told him and turned around, facing the water once again.

Just as the waves came up and washed away the footprints in the sand, he removed the pain from her heart and she just loved everything about him.

Ugh, Farren loved and hated "the beginning stage". It had a way of causing you to feel emotions you never felt. Farren was so happy lately, it bothered her.

She wiped a few tears that fell from her face, Jonte wrapped his arms around her waist. "You love me boo?" he whispered in her ear and kissed her neck.

"You been knew that," she mumbled and wiped her face again.

"I love you more," he told her, holding her tight. He said it again, "I love you so much." Farren smiled, her heart smiled, her soul smiled. The love angels were full of praise. Whoever said a broken heart doesn't heal never gave theirs the chance to mend.

Farren wiped her tears, pulled away from Jonte and left.

She got a message from one of those text free apps, the only way she knew it was a text free app, was because it had a plus sign in front of the first number. "You should have never left. Tsk, tsk."

Farren didn't know what that meant, she had been at the elevator waiting impatiently for a few minutes, and she kept pressing the button to bring the cart up to get her. She needed to get her children from her mom's house and ask her mom where she could go.

Farren threw her cell phone in the trash, she was tired of people calling and texting her. She just wanted all of this shit to end.

"Crash cart in room six right now, code red, code red, code red!" a nurse yelled into the phone and slammed it down running back down the hall.

Farren prayed for whoever it is…then she thought, "Room six?"

Room six…Room six…that was Jonte's room. Her heart dropped as she took off running down the hallway. There was a nurse charging his sides to get his heart beating once again.

"Ma'am you cannot be in here," another nurse told her.

"Please save him! Oh my! Please do whatever you can," she cried and begged, she tried her hardest to get around the lady. Farren needed him to hear her voice, smell her scent, so that he could know he was not able to die on her. She was planning on coming to get him in the morning, there was no way she was living life without her man by her side. It took a lot of shit to happen for her to realize that Jonte was the one, she refused to leave him.

"It's over, call it," the doctor told the nurse.

"Over?" she asked, vision blurry, because pain and anxiety had filled her eyes.

"Time of death, 21:46." The nurse looked at the clock and another documented it.

Farren walked over to him and told them to get the fuck out.

"What happened baby?"

"Baby, what happened?"

"Who did this to you?" she asked.

"Baby…you left me, you promised me your last name," she cried, over his dead body.

Someone was on to her ass, like white on rice.

Farren cried and kissed his face for as long as they allowed her too, the nurses asked her was there anyone she could call to come get her, but she told them no.

Farren was pissed the fuck off, she sat in her Range Rover until the sun came up in the hospital deck. She was sure her mother had been blowing her phone up, but she didn't care. Well, she couldn't think.

She had literally lost every single person that meant something to her, every single man died. Farren couldn't stop shaking and crying. She heard a phone vibrate, what phone was it. She threw her iPhone away.

It vibrated again, and again, and again. She exhaled and got the phone out of her purse. Farren answered the phone because she knew there wasn't any more bad news that could break her at this point.

The families could call all day every day. She had already decided to vote for Greg, so she could live in peace.

"I hated to do that to you Farren, I really did," a voice came over the phone.

"Kim?" Farren asked, she knew it was her because she had tons of conversations before with her, conversations about shopping, eating, traveling and life in general.

"I had to kill him before Mario did. See, even with me fucking Bianchi and telling him all of the Sanchez family business, I still don't think he wanted me to be head of The Cartel," she told her.

"Kim, fuck you!" she yelled.

"I never did anything to you," she said in anger.

Kim said, "You're absolutely right, which is why you should just vote for me. Farren come on now, don't act like you're going to really miss Jonte. I know you were fucking Kool," she said.

That hurt more than anything to even bring Kool up at a time like this, but what Farren failed to realize was that in The Cartel, feelings didn't matter. No one cared about how you felt or what hurt your feelings or made you feel some type of way.

"I'll be expecting your vote darling. Don't forget that I've been to your home, I've met your mother, your sister in Houston, even your amazing stepmother out in Cali," she said laughing and hanging the phone up.

Farren was so angry, she banged her head on the steering wheel until it bled and it hurt so bad she had to stop. Farren leaned back in pain, she was so angry. There weren't any words to describe just how she was feeling.

 Christian Knight told her that this would happened, Farren now hated her stupid fucking father. Why would he do this to her? Why would he drag her into this life, knowing the repercussions, what kind of dad would do this to her? What had she ever done to live such a miserable life, she just lost someone else near and dear to her. Farren was just over everything, but her children would keep her fighting.

Just not right now, Farren couldn't be around with anyone. She didn't even know how she was going to deliver more bad news to her kids, like she just couldn't.

Farren decided that they would have to stay with her mom tonight, she just needed one night to cry and mourn. She went to the liquor store where everyone stared. She had a big ass knot on her head, her eyes were swollen, hair all over head, and her clothes were wrinkled. An observer would have thought, that she was jumped or worse involved in a domestic abuse situation. Farren ordered a pint of Patron and took her ass home.

She sat in the living room, with the old Jodeci album on repeat, she drunk out the bottle and smoked weed all night.

Farren was going through it honey, she was really going through it.

She had no cell phone, no husband, no first love, no best friend, no baby daddy, and no boyfriend. She just felt miserable. What had she done so wrong to receive such karma in her life, back to back?

Farren stumbled to her basement and went through a few dusty boxes looking for pictures of her and Dice. She tore them all up. "I hate you, you fucking bastard," she cried and shouted.

Why was Farren blaming Dice when she knew he was married? Who was Farren to blame a man for things were going wrong in her life, for Christian cheating on her and leaving her for a stripper, for her father not really caring about her… just using her as a pawn in his little sick game, for Jonte who loved her so much to the point where he felt the need to seek attention elsewhere because she stopped taking caring of home? She blamed Dice for her killing Kool. Her mind was fucked up at the same time and she took her anger out on him and killed his ass.

Farren needed someone to blame, she would never admit that she needed to learn how to be alone and love herself.

She could never openly say, I don't like being alone. I thrive off of attention and company.

As sad as it sounds, God does everything for a reason and He was really trying to show her something.

Too bad, Farren would never be able to learn the lesson…

Chapter Thirteen

"Wake up," she told her, smacking her face as hard as she could. She didn't even have to be so rough, but because she had always been a bad bitch and she never just seen her looking pitiful, down bad, or ugly. She felt the need to treat her as she has always treated her in the past, like she was nothing, gum on the bottom of a shoe, a prostitute and sadly the help. She had always done all she could to love her and be her friend, but it was never enough. Farren never made her feel welcomed, she always had something slick to say, something rude or disrespectful.

But today, this bitch was about to die.

Farren came to her senses, "Mari?" she asked, rubbing the side of her face.

"Hoe, you know this is me. Get your ass up," she told her.

Farren acted like she was about to roll over and stand up, but when she stood she punched the shit out of Mari.

"Oh you wanna fight?" she asked.

"Girl bring it please, I need to release some anger. Come on hoe," Farren yelled. She really was hungover like hell and her head was banging. Farren would be damned if she let a hoe catch her slipping, she had went through too much shit this year to go out like a sucker.

Mari came at her and Farren punched her again, blood started gushing her out of her nose.

"Aah," she bent over and moaned.

Farren kicked her in her stomach. "You reallyyyyyyy thought you was about to come in my house and kill me? You better get up and fight me," she kicked her again.

Farren was pumped up now, she wasn't with the shit today and poor little Mari was about to get it.

Mari tried to stand, but Farren dragged her by her hair to the light in the basement so she could see and she stomped her out.

Before she could continue, a gun shot rang out.

Farren wondered who the fuck was in her house.

This was some bullshit, there was no way that someone else was invading her personal space. All she wanted was to mourn Jonte's death in peace.

But it didn't look like that was about to happen.

"I don't have time for this shit," Greg said, standing up from where he was sitting on the couch. He scared the hell out of her. She damn sure wasn't expecting to see him, but it wasn't a surprise. Money and power made people do some fucked up shit.

He got closer and shot Mari in the head, she was already damn near passed out on the floor anyway.

Farren tried to run but Greg was so close to her, and she was kind of frozen.

"Greg," Farren pleaded.

"Shut up," he told her.

"She hated you so much, it was so easy to get her to be on my side, got Jonte back in the game, and like a dummy you just kept giving her money... I done bought a few whips off her husband money, I ain't even gone lie," he said, smiling.

"Then when I tipped the FEDS on their trap at the house, it just kept getting better," he continued.

Farren wondered who made him so angry. When did he become like this? Her heart was beating so fast.

"I'm going to vote for you, I promise," she told him.

"Farren, let me tell you what I put together," he leaned on the pool table.

"You are The Cartel," he said and looked at her in her eyes.

"That nigga Jeff, I had to kill his ass because he knew what Bianchi was planning to do the whole time."

Farren's eyes got big, he killed Jeff that day. It wasn't Bianchi.

Farren wasn't feeling none of this news at all. How was she was supposed to carry The Cartel? She was a woman. A woman had never led The Cartel or so she thought...

Greg continued, "He peeped it a long time ago. I was listening on one of his phone calls and I still don't know who he was on the phone with... I ain't figured it out yet, but I heard him say, she's almost ready and she's going to change the game."

"You were always going to die... I hate to say this, but I thought why just kill her and leave all of these people here to miss you. So I did you a favor and eliminated all of em for you," he told her.

Farren shook her head. "You're a liar," she told him, crying.

Why was this happening to her? Farren couldn't believe she was about to die, her children were about to be parentless. Her life wasn't supposed to end like this, she didn't spend all of that time in law school, and enduring all of life's battles to go out like this…it was so unfair.

"Please do not kill me," she begged. Farren had never begged for anything in her life, she didn't believe that people deserved that much out of her. Ever since a little girl, she told herself that anything she want she could get, that attitude carried her from a little girl to a grown woman with a successful career and three children, a marriage. Farren experienced a lot, she had done a lot wrong, things she would never dare to repeat to anyone. But overall, her life wasn't over, her book wasn't supposed to end like this.

Farren didn't agree with the way this selfish fucker was handling this, there had to be something that she could do.

"Greg!" she went towards him.

Greg pointed his gun to her. "Shut up and get back, I'm talking to you," he told her.

Farren took a deep breath, her head was hurting so bad and then Mari's body had started to stink. She really wanted to throw up.

"So, as I was saying, before you interrupted me… Bianchi wanted you to pick your own second in command, that's why your vote mattered so much," he said.

Farren refused to even process the bullshit. "See, I'm tired of being second. I've been second for years, so I gotta kill you. Sorry boo," he told her and knocked her upside the head before she could even realize what happened. Greg was sure that blow killed her, he cracked his knuckles and went up the stairs.

He was about to leave, he got in his car, drove through the subdivision to prepare to head to Miami, when he remembered what someone great told him, "Always make sure you kill em."

Greg backtracked into the house quietly and that's when he saw Farren slowly crawling up the steps, the side of her face was bleeding like crazy.

See what Greg didn't know was that Farren turned her shoulder when she saw that his foot was moving towards her. She just knew that he was going to shoot her ass up, but when he walked away she was so grateful.

Although, she was slipping in and out of consciousness, she just needed to get to a phone and call 911.

Farren was so out of it, barely making it up the stairs, her body was in excruciating pain.

"Gotcha," Greg said. Farren looked up, vision super blurry and one bullet sent her tumbling down the steps.

Farren Knight died instantly.

The Funeral

Noel leaned on her grandmother for support. She sat in this same church at her sister's funeral, her father's funeral, her Auntie Courtney's funeral, and just a few days prior at her second dad, Jonte's funeral. She couldn't imagine ever burying her mother. She wasn't prepared for this, she was only ten years old and she had no parents. Noel couldn't stop crying, she just wanted this day to be over. She got up to use the restroom, she just needed a few seconds to herself.

Her Auntie Neeki asked her, "Where are you going baby?"

"To the bathroom," she whispered.

"I'll go with you," she whispered back.

"I'll take her, I need a cigarette," Mrs. Nakia said. She didn't cry, she just didn't but Lord knows her heart was hurting.

Noel and her granny took the middle aisle to the bathroom. Everyone whispered, "That's her daughter," "No, not the oldest, remember they found her head on somebody's porch," "That's the other one," they all whispered.

Noel wiped more tears. To the left of her, she saw this lady who looked just like her mom, well not really, but she had her mother's chinky eyes and full lips.

That lady looked like her mama! Noel felt for a moment that was her mama.

She pulled on her grandmother. "Look, there go my mama," she said loudly.

People in the funeral looked towards the middle aisle, while Mrs. Nakia jerked Noel's arm. "Come on chile and be quiet," she told her, but not before looking at the young woman who Noel felt was her mom.

After Noel tinkled and washed her hands, her grandmother told her to go back into the church, when she saw Bianchi sitting down on a bench surrounded by his henchmen.

"Move out of my damn way," she said loudly, cursing in the church and all she didn't care.

"She's cool, let her be," he told them.

"Nakia, how you been?" he asked.

"Fuck you! What is that girl doing here?" she whispered.

Bianchi looked up at her. "What girl? What are you talking about?" he asked, confused.

Mrs. Nakia took off her hat and her shades and bent down to meet Bianchi's eyes, beer and cigarette breath. She said, "CHANEL CAVETT!"

The End.

Made in the USA
Columbia, SC
06 August 2019